The Love
She
Longed For

SERIES

MY LOVE
WON'T LAST
Forever
HIS WIFE
3

JAHZARA BRADLEY

My Love Won't Last Forever 3: HIS WIFE

ISBN 978-0-9882794-9-0

Library of Congress Number 2017910812

Cover Design: Donna Osborn Clark at
www.CreationByDonna.com

Layout and Interior Design: CreationsByDonna@gmail.com

Published by: Tranquil Moments

TRANQUIL
MOMENTS

Printed in the United States of America

Acknowledgments

Thank you to my wonderful friends and family who have supported past book endeavors and encouraged me on this journey. I wish my best friend, Candi were here to see how this one unfolded. Rest in heaven, Candi. I'm sure you would think I did the story justice.

To my mother, who told me on one cold winter day in 2013, to do what makes me happy and do me. Writing always makes me happy and I did it.

To my sister, Jen, who has been with me since day one of this journey when this book started in a blue spiral notebook and moved to scrap pieces of papers, text messages, three or four other notebooks.

To Dat Dude for giving me such rich material to work with.

To Rob-G, whom I've been cool with since Fall '91 at Indiana University Bloomington. I know you didn't believe me when I said I finished the book, but this is proof I did it. Oh and you got to read the entire book because I did put you in here.

To my homeboy, my locker partner in high school, Ellis, thank you so much for being Ellis! Thank you for allowing me to use 50

Shades of Gold how I wanted to, those were you words. And I hope you like my spin on Onyx Green.

To my writing mentor, Dominique Watson, thank you so much for helping me get my writing juices to flow again. I'm on that next level…

To my readers thank you so much for your patience. I know you all have been waiting for more of Malachi and Nyree. This is it for them. They are now going into retirement. They may do cameo appearances in other books but they're mid-forties now and can't be doing all that drama and chaos.

To my daughters, Amber and Halle, it is my hope that you will discover your gifts and talents and set the world ablaze with them.

PROLOGUE

Ivan Marrick IV had planned to be at home long before nine o'clock at night. His day had started out running a few errands, and he'd lost track of time. He drew in a breath and told himself there was nothing to fear as he allowed his BMW 750i to roll into his driveway. Pressing the remote to his garage opener he prayed that the garage door would lift with a push of the button. *You've got to conquer your fear. Damn, I wished I would have gotten here at eight o'clock. I'm not going there,* he thought to himself. Although he told himself he was not going to go back to the dreadful ordeal that occurred twenty years ago, his mind decided he should revisit it.

After rolling the BMW 750i into the driveway, Charity Marrick gently placed her foot onto the brake as she nudged her son on the shoulder to awaken him.

"Ivan. Ivan, come on and get up. We're home now. Boy, I know you can't be that tired. All you did during Bible Study was homework and sleep. Come on boy and get up."

He heard her and was trying to wake up, but he was tired. Every night they were going to somebody's church for some function. He loved God, but he was tired. Most nights they didn't make it home until nine or ten o'clock. He had to wake up at five o'clock in the morning so that he had enough time to eat, shower, and make the thirty-minute commute to his private school.

This morning his homeroom teacher threatened to call Division of Family and Children Services if he fell asleep one more time in class. Ivan recalled Mrs. Lattimore saying something about his mother being an unfit mother. He wanted to lash out at Mrs. Lattimore, but he knew that his mother didn't need anything else to worry about. Ivan knew his mother was doing the best she could. People called on the phone constantly about money. When the one-eight-hundred numbers came up on the caller ID screen, she told him not to answer.

He said, "Okay."

He was eight years old, so he did what he was told. She was worried about his dad who hadn't been home in over a week. Ivan finally opened his eyes, looked at the clock in the car, and saw it was nine o'clock. He saw his mother reach over and press the garage opener, but nothing happened. *I hope our electricity is not off again. It was the last time the garage wouldn't go up. No, that can't be. The lights are on in the house.* Again and again, she pressed the button, and still no movement of the garage door.

Finally, she sighed and said, "Okay Son, we have to be aware of our surroundings. Look around. It looks good. Now on the count of three, get out the car. You run to the garage door and lift up, and I will pull in."

Ivan did as instructed. Once Charity pulled in, he let the door down. Both Ivan and Charity approached the door to enter the house. They both felt electric volts from a stun gun pulsate through their bodies before they were stuffed into the backseat of Charity's foreign car. Their kidnappers took them to an underground hideaway on the site of Marrick Construction. It was dark and dank inside.

"Ma, I know where we are," Ivan told Charity. She was weak and tired.

"Ivan, what have I told you about lying. If you lie, you steal, and if you steal, you kill. Little boy, I'm not raising a liar. Shut up."

"Ma, I think we can get out of here. I've been in here before. Daddy showed me this place and told me about it."

"Umph," was all she could muster saying as she laid on her back. She had crawled around on her knees earlier trying to figure out how to get out, and there was no sign of entry. Her husband was a master craftsman and there was probably a way out, but she couldn't figure it out. Stretching out as best she could, her foot kicked a person.

"Sorry, Ivan, what are you doing under my feet? I thought you were behind me."

"Ma, my head is touching your head. I'm not under you."

"Okay," Charity mumbled as she brought herself to her knees and reached down to where her feet had been. She felt around in the dark until her hand touched something hairy. Allowing her hand to follow down the head, touching the ear and then onto the neck, she realized she was touching a cold body.

"Ma, we got to get out of here. I can't breathe and that smell. I can't take it anymore, it's going to kill us. Have you ever smelled something like this in your life?"

"No, Son. No, I haven't. The LORD is my shepherd, I shall not want. He maketh me to lie down in green pastures, he leadeth me beside the still waters. He restoreth my soul," Charity said.

"Ma, do you think Daddy is going to pay those men their money? They said if he doesn't pay up in forty-eight hours, it's going to be ashes to ashes and dust to dust for us. I don't think they're going to kill us. They've given us food and stuff."

"Baby, I believe they are not playing. Here, let's scoot back over here," she told him and held onto him tightly.

"I'm scared Mom. Do you think Daddy is going to pay?"

"The Lord will make a way for our escape," she told her son.

The entrance door opened, and the man who did most of the talking and threatening was there. Ivan recognized his cologne. He spoke with a slightly southern dialect, almost making it hard to understand.

"Today's your lucky day. Ivan came through for you all. Don't know where he got the money, but he got it with interest. He should've never run off with my dope and not paid me. Here's how this is going to go. My mans here is going to put y'all back into the car, and when you wake up, you're going to go home and live life like normal. If you go to the police, I will find you and kill you. Your mother is in that nice senior living home. I paid her a visit the other day. We had a nice time chatting about you, her favorite daughter. It's kind of messed up with you being a twin, but every family has its dysfunction. Anyway, if you go to the police, I will torture her and kill her, like I did your cellmate over there. I got to get him out of here, he's stinking up the place. Enough chatting, y'all be safe out there in these streets. It's a cold mean world out there."

****

Ivan sighed a sigh of relief when the garage door went up. On the count of three, he hopped out of the car, approached his entrance door, disabled the alarm system to his house, and entered without incident.

Soap Opera Poem - Jahzara Bradley

I've been Young and Restless,

And sometimes reckless.

All the Days of My Life,

I've never seen the righteous forsaken.

Even though, my heart's achin' and breakin.

In my Search for Tomorrow.

When I thought to beg, steal, and borrow.

I didn't know how I would cope.

But He's always been Jahzara's reason for hope.

Some days have been darker than a thousand midnights.

Yet He's been my Guiding Light.

ABC, CBS, and NBC will sho' nuf give you the blues.

You had better pick up the Bible…NIV

To read the good news.

MALACHI CHANDLER

Following behind the hostess, Rayna Summers sashayed her five-foot-eight frame to the table where her boyfriend of the past two years, Malachi Chandler awaited her. Malachi couldn't help but notice that the striped black and white dress she wore accentuated her voluptuous hips. When she leaned over to kiss him on the cheek, he got a nice view of well-endowed bosom and seeing her tattoo of the strawberry dipped in whip cream sent a ripple through his body. She smiled as she gently stroked his jaw. His charcoal complexion next to her caramel hand blended well. "Hey Baby, I'm here," she smiled. While he enjoyed seeing her smile and found her smile to be soothing, it would not save her from Malachi's wrath. As soon as the hostess departed, Malachi started in on Rayna. "Damn, Rayna, I said three not four," Malachi snapped as he looked at his Rado Jubile timepiece and watched Rayna take a seat across from him at his favorite restaurant, Cooper's Hawk Winery.

Rayna tossed her hair and looked around to see if anyone she knew was in the vicinity. Even though she was not at work, she was always looking for a story or someone to interview on her cable network station. Slightly annoyed by Malachi's unresponsiveness to her affection, she rolled her eyes and looked at her matching Rado timepiece.

"You are so hyperbolic. I mean you exaggerate all the time. I see you, Bae, you're looking good with the fresh taper. Uh-oh, you're wearing the Purple Label Ralph Lauren. You're looking real good," she said licking her lips in a seductive manner. Rayna looked into Malachi's round, dark brown eyes and noticed that they were piercing her. She let out a sigh as she noticed his eyes drifted back to his watch. She continued, "It's 3:45. It is not four o'clock." As she observed some of the patrons drinking and laughing loudly, she thought that it might be later than mid-afternoon.

"Rayna, three-forty-five is damn near four o'clock. It sure in the hell ain't three o'clock," he huffed. His skin was charcoal and smooth except for the vein that was going to burst in his forehead.

"Traffic was a bitch," she lied. Rayna tossed her hair again and smiled. A gesture that often allowed her to get her way with Malachi.

"You are such a liar. Damn, Rayna, just stop it," Malachi sipped from his glass and put it down. He shook his head in disgust. "I'm not a priority in your life. Everything comes before me, especially your precious television studio that you wouldn't have if it weren't for me." Malachi felt relieved as he released his feelings. It hadn't been his intent for the date to turn into an argument. He ran his hand across his six pack as if to see if they were still there. *I've been drinking a lot lately. I sure hope all the hidden sugar in these drinks don't cause me to add inches to my stomach, I work too hard in the gym to sabotage my hard work,* he found himself thinking.

It was apparent his attitude was starting to wear on her nerves. "I'm really not in the mood for this shit today, Malachi. I thought we were having date night today at least that's what you said in your text."

"You are so out of touch with us. When's the last time we had date night? I'll wait." He sat with his fingers intertwined staring at her round face which was starting to show signs of aging. He had never noticed it until now. *Damn, I wonder if I'm starting to age.*

Rayna shrugged her shoulders, "I give up…"

Her nonchalant attitude had added fuel to the fire. "Me too. I give up. I can't do this anymore. In fact, I don't want to do this anymore. " His shoulders relaxed. It was as if tension were leaving his body.

"What?" she asked in an irritated tone. You can't be serious; because I can't remember our last date night," Rayna hunched her shoulders and looked around trying to see if anyone might be listening to their conversation. Northwest Indiana was a very small place and gossip traveled quicker than the speed of lightning.

"Oh, she finally made it," the waitress said while looking and half-smiling at Malachi, "can I get you something?" she asked directing her attention to Rayna. Taking a second glance at Rayna while taking her notepad and pen out of her apron, the waitress gasped, "You're, you're," she snapped her fingers, "Rayna Summers. I watch your talk show, "Keeping It 100" Can I get a selfie with you? I already took one with Mr. Chandler."

"Yes, sure you can, Bae, take it with my phone too," Rayna said as she entered the password and handed her phone to him. After the picture, Rayna took her seat and turned to the young woman and said, "Let me have a glass of Blueberry wine to start with. I haven't looked at the menu yet,"

"Sure take your time. Mr. Chandler, are you ready to order?"

"I'm fine. I'm going to have another Corona with lime and some grenadine."

"Okay, I will put that in for you," the waitress said as she disappeared.

"Rayna, look, I got to be honest with you, a couple of months ago when you asked me if I was still feeling this relationship, I lied and said yes. Truth is I've been going through the motions, and I just want to be happy. I'm not happy."

"Really, Malachi. That's bullshit. All of sudden you're not happy," she sniffed trying to hold back tears.

Malachi sat across from his girlfriend of the past two years with no emotion. He felt nothing for her. While she was beautiful, sexy, and intelligent, she no longer made his heart skip a beat. His heart belonged to his ex-wife, Nyree and that's who he wanted to be with.

"You know I like to give it to you straight no chaser. I've been spending a lot of time with Nyree and the kids lately, and I've decided that I want my family back. You know I've invested in the television studio, but that's yours to do as you please."

At the very center of her being, Rayna was hurt and devastated. "So, let me get this right," Rayna swallowed. Drawing in a breath and allowing it to leave her nostrils slowly, she paused and then spoke, "Malachi, you're leaving me for your ex-wife? That's bullshit. You're a bullshit assed ni…" He had almost made her go there with him. He smiled a sinister grin. His smile was one of his best assets, and he worked it like a charm. Malachi knew that Rayna was trying to keep her composure because they were in public. She had spoken many times about the "n" word being a harmful word and that she would not ever let it flow off her lips. *Hypocrite,* he found himself thinking at her near slip.

He recalled her having said in a previous conversation about how demeaning the word had been to their ancestors. "The music, culture, and society had made it perfectly acceptable to use the racial epithet," she had once told him. He recalled having said to her, "You sure don't mind spending the money that I make saying it in rap songs." Malachi sat there in silence with a smirk on his face that indicated everything she said was correct. His demeanor suggested he had nothing to lose.

Her light complexion was turning red. She imagined that she was beet red as she absently watched the waitress set her glass in front of her. It didn't take much for her fair skin to turn red.

"Here's your Blueberry wine," the waitress interrupted as she placed the glass in front of Rayna, then turning to Malachi she said, "Here's your Corona with lime and a hint of grenadine, Mr. Chandler? Can I get you all anything else?"

As Rayna raised her glass to her lips and took a sip of her drink, she gave him a look that said, "I dare you to say I'm right."

Flashing his million dollar smile, he said, "No, I'm good." The look on his face said he was preoccupied and had better things to do than continuing to sit and drink.

"Okay, just holler if you need something," she said flirtingly as she sauntered off.

Rayna rolled her eyes in disbelief. There was a sense of flirtation in the air. Malachi had given the waitress a look to suggest interest. He was a man. He looked. He admired beauty, but she was not his type. Only one woman had him preoccupied, and it was not Rayna. Refocusing his attention on Rayna, no words were exchanged, but the look he gave her said, "You're damned right." After the long silence, he spoke. He shrugged his shoulders to indicate that he really didn't care how she might be feeling at the time. In fact, he encouraged himself to continue divulging his feelings.

"Rayna, it was fun," he cupped his goatee and let his hand drop to his lap. Slowly speaking as if he were checking his mind for the correct words to say," I wouldn't take back the past two years, but we both know that you never wanted me for me. You wanted what you could get. You're an opportunist, and I gave you an opportunity. Now the ride is over. You get to walk away with more than you've ever had."

"What?" Rayna fumed. "I'm appalled that you're talking to me in this manner. Let you tell it I'm a gold digger. It almost sounds like I'm a prostitute or something. Is that what you think of me? You act like I've been exchanging sex for goods? If that's the case what does that say about you? Hmph?"

Malachi picked up his beer and took a deep swallow, sat his glass down and stared at Rayna. He winked at her. The media had pegged him as a womanizer. If he were honest with himself, he might agree with the stereotype.

No longer able to contain her anger, she threw the drink at him. Rayna had never been athletically inclined. When she played darts, she had never been able to hit the bull's eye. Bull's eye would have been Malachi's face. As usual, she missed her intended target. Half of the contents in the glass splattered on his tailor-fitted Pique Polo from the Ralph Lauren Purple Label collection. Although it was not his smooth as a baby's behind face, she was pleased the drink landed on his shirt. He prided himself on his Ralph Lauren Black and Purple Label collection items, and she had just ruined one of his prized possessions. True, he could get another shirt, but she took pleasure in knowing she would be the cause of him having to replace the acid green Polo. This shirt had been ordered offline and not purchased in a department store so replacing it might be next to impossible.

Malachi gasped as he looked down at his shirt. Shaking his head in disgust, he drew his full lips in tightly, released them, raised his hand and hit the table hard. Finally, he responded, "You know what Rayna, that was real childish. You only did that shit because we're in public. I've never hit a woman or been violent toward a woman in my life. You, my dear, are about to become an exception to the rule. Just know if we weren't in this bar, I would choke the shit out of you, real talk. I put that on everything I love. I put that on my grandma. I really don't know how I've tolerated you this long. Yep, that's what I'm saying. I'm going back to my family. I know I've invested in the television studio, but it's yours to do as you please. ." He stood up and reached into his front pocket and exclaimed, "Look, I gotta run! But here's a couple of hundred dollars. Feel free to continue to drink since I'm wearing most of your drink." He laughed heartily and continued making suggestions, "Have dinner or whatever. It's on me and be sure to tip the waitress nicely."

"Hmm," she sneered. "Malachi, you're definitely going to pay in more ways than one." He got up, walked out of the restaurant and never looked back.

Rayna looked at the four crisp one-hundred dollar bills scattered on the table and whispered, "Malachi, you're definitely going to pay in more ways than one." A tear dropped from her right eye as she raised her near empty wine glass to her lips as she watched him walk out of her life.

Speeding out of the parking lot seemed like a great idea when he hopped into his black Range Rover. However, as he approached Luke's gas station at the corner of U.S. Route 30 and Mississippi Street, the two Merrillville Police cars that pulled him over didn't seem to share his sentiments. *Where did these bastards come from? They had to have been lurking in the cut,* Malachi found himself thinking.

"Dammit," Malachi said dryly as he reached for his license and registration. He banged his right hand on the steering wheel three times.

I must be a magnet for the police. I seem to attract these bastards everywhere I go. What the hell is wrong with me? I need an encounter with the police like I need a hole in my head. I can't believe this. First, Rayna's hysterics in Cooper's Hawk. Why did she have to throw her drink on me? That's all I need is a DUI. These bastards are going to swear up and down I'm drunk. Of course, I smell of alcohol, the heifer just tossed a drink on me, and my breath is going to smell of beer. If it ain't one damn thing, it's another. Now Merrillville police are behind me. They always come in droves when they pull a brother over. I just want to make it home safely and go to sleep, but something tells me this day is about to get longer than what I anticipated.

By the time the officer made it to the driver's side, Malachi was handing his license and registration out of the window, with his right hand on the steering wheel. He didn't want the officer to think he was reaching for a weapon that he didn't even have or trying to be confrontational. It could be dangerous for an African-American male to be Driving While Black. The routine was all too familiar. He'd been pulled over enough times to know the drill. One might even call him a habitual traffic offender.

"Sir, do you know how fast you were going?" Officer Morrison asked.

Malachi sighed. *Let the bullshit begin. Here we go,* he thought to himself. This was beginning to feel like Murphy's Law. Anything that could go wrong would go wrong. Hadn't that been the story of his life? Nyree was always telling him to speak positive mantras, think positive thoughts and he would attract the things he wanted. It was not working. All he wanted was to have a life with Nyree, the love of his life. It seemed like it was always one obstacle after another. All he could do now was shake his head at the officer to indicate he didn't know how fast he was going. More importantly, he found himself thinking, *how much is this going to cost me? I sure hope they don't hope to ask to search the car. There was a small amount of marijuana in a dime bag under the driver's seat. It's barely enough to roll a joint.*

His cell phone rang and his eighteen-year-old daughter's million dollar smiling face, which she inherited from him, flashed across the screen. She looked like a younger, thinner, and lighter complexion version of her mother. His heart began pounding. Not only was he concerned about Nyree he began thinking about his children, India and Christian.

Letting out a sigh, he felt like he screwed up again. Most people would get a slap on the wrist or a ticket for one hundred fifty dollars. But because he had bad luck with the police, he was sure this would probably be a thousand dollar ticket and, if he was lucky, he would be able to drive away without getting beaten for something they mistakenly thought he was doing.

Finally, the phone stopped ringing, and Malachi answered the officer, "Uh, no Sir, I don't really know how fast I was going. I just got a call from my daughter, and her tutoring session let out early, and she's stranded at the school. In fact, that was her calling just a second ago. I just hope she's not standing out in the cold," he lied. Malachi couldn't remember the last time he had picked his children up from school. For the past two years, both children had matching BMWs and had been driving themselves to school. When it was rough weather Christian, his son was the designated driver. India hated it, but that was the rule. The alternative was she could catch the school bus. Malachi snickered as he recalled hearing India say, "I'll have my own Uber transport me before I get on a school bus."

The officer looked at his license and said, "Malachi Chandler as in the rapper?"

Looking puzzled, he looked at the thin black man in the police uniform. "Yes," he responded nervously. Police and rappers usually are not on the same side of the fence. Malachi was convinced he was getting ready to get hit with all kind of erroneous charges.

The officer asked, "What school does your daughter attend?"

"Wirt-Emerson Visual and Performing Arts Academy," Malachi responded not really sure why the officer would even ask and hoping that he was not going to try to verify that lie he just told.

"Oh, okay, my son attends Wirt-Emerson as well. He's a huge fan. He's never going to believe that I met you. You better slow down out here. We're slated to get three to four inches of snow tonight, I bet that will slow you down," he chuckled.

Malachi simply nodded his head. He had no intentions of being out when the snow began to hit the ground. If he had his way, he would be at home in front of the fireplace with a nice adult beverage.

The officer became serious again as he spoke, Look, I could ticket you for excessive speed. I ran your plates. You know if you get one more ticket your license could be suspended? "

Again Malachi nodded. Malachi was hoping this cop was not getting ready to try to extort some money from him. He had about eight hundred dollars in cash on him, and he was not trying to have to pay this guy off. However, the officer's tone insinuated that Malachi's excessive speed was getting ready to cost him something.

"My son, Brodie, is having his sixteenth birthday party Friday night at seven at the Avalon. If you could make an appearance we can forget about this whole situation."

Malachi squinted, a gesture he often made when he heard something, but was not sure if he had heard it correctly. "Okay," Malachi responded without much zeal. He didn't need any bad press at this moment, and Nyree would have a fit if she found out about this incident. He was forty-five years old and too old to be without a legitimate driver's license. This officer could be a jerk and make him do a breathalyzer. He had been drinking heavily all day and had smoked a blunt too. He wanted all negative situations to disappear, and this was a small cost. *I need to get my life together. I'm out here in these streets acting like I'm still in my twenties. I'm way too old for this mess. I could be in the back of a squad car right now for some bull shit. How would I explain this to my teenage children, especially Christian who we grounded from driving because of drunk driving on New Year's Eve? Bottom line I gotta quit doing dumb shit, point blank and period.*

"And one more thing, can you step out of the vehicle and take a picture with me?"

"Okay, I guess," Malachi responded reluctantly. This whole encounter was getting more bizarre by the moment. He felt even weirder standing six foot four next to the officer, who had to be around Nyree's height, five foot four. After taking the picture, he watched Officer Morrison and the other police car drive off. He turned onto I-65 and drove to his home in Miller Beach. He was very careful to stay in the slow lane and drive exactly fifty-five miles per hour. When he walked through the door of his beach front home, the phone rang and it was India.

"Daddy, can you bring me something to eat?"

"Yeah, Baby Girl," he told his eighteen-year-old daughter, "where is your mom?" He didn't feel like leaving his home. Why couldn't India have called like ten minutes ago? He didn't complain, though. After all, she was part of the reason he didn't get arrested. The small lie he told about going to pick her up from school had really helped him out with Officer Morrison.

"Daddy, you know her business is *her* business. Can you bring me something to eat and oh, by the way, bring Bruh Bruh something to eat too? I am not going to share any of my food with him."

"Okay," Malachi chuckled.

"What's so funny?"

"India, nothing, I'm just tripping that you're still calling him Bruh Bruh after all this time." Malachi's mind flashed back to the day that Bruh Bruh had come into their lives.

****

Nyree had just left a doctor's appointment and in her opinion, she had received a death sentence. She had rushed over to Malachi's home to vent to him. Under normal circumstances, she would not have used the key he had given her to let herself in, but this situation was far from normal. She had gone through her ex-husband's home shouting out to him, and when she didn't get a response, she went to the section of the home that housed the studio. Malachi had been in the studio with Aris Smith, who was Nyree's former best friend. She had financed Aris's day spa; Tranquil Moments. Aris betrayed her trust by taking the finances to open a strip club. Nyree became furious and pulled the plug on her best friend's sinking business.

It just happened. And the day Nyree came to Malachi's studio uninvited, she heard her former best friend and ex-husband laughing, moaning and groaning.

At the time, Aris was drowning in financial woes and Malachi was drowning in his own sorrows. Nyree had miscarried Malachi's baby but failed to mention to him that she was pregnant. Malachi felt she had withheld the information to hurt him. No matter how many times she tried to tell him she had only known she had been pregnant for a week or so and then miscarried, Malachi couldn't accept her words as truth. To get revenge, he purchased Tranquil Moments and changed the name to Chaotic Bliss. It had never been his intention to have an affair with Aris. When Malachi realized Nyree was in the house, he ran to the door of the studio, and he refused to let Nyree in.

"Nyree, I'm in the process of laying this track down," he lied and didn't realize the recording light was not illuminated. Thinking she had fallen for the lie, he continued, "I will come by your place in about an hour." As he walked her down the hall to the main house, Aris called his name. He remembered trying to hurry Nyree along while praying she didn't recognize the voice.

"Who is that?" Nyree questioned.

He attempted to avoid answering truthfully by saying, "I don't ask you about your business dealings so don't do that to me, Nyree." His prayers went unanswered when Aris appeared within steps behind them.

"I see," Nyree said to Malachi who was staring at Aris in an agitated manner.

Dead wrong and caught in a compromising situation, Malachi said, "I really hope you're not about to start tripping."

Nyree's tone had been calm. "I'm not about to trip? Why would I? My ex-husband and ex-best friend are screwing each other behind my back. There is no need to trip about that, right? Everybody in Gary has been talking about it for months, but today I get to see it for myself."

Aris interjected, "Whatever, Nyree you don't know what you're talking about."

Malachi spoke, "Aris, please, I got this. Nyree, I told you I was handling business."

Nyree shook her head. "You're right. You did tell me you were handling business. Aris, you've always been good at handling my left-overs. You always got my hand-me-downs and no matter how hard you tried, you could never seem to really make them yours. They just never seemed to look like they belonged to you. Malachi, this is so classic of you. I would expect nothing less of you!" Nyree had shouted before storming out of his home. Her reaction had been normal under the circumstances, but Malachi recalled thinking that there was a strange look about her. There was a dark shadow about her person. A few moments later he would get a phone call from her saying she had been speeding down the block and hit a kid in the street. The parents would later lose custody of the child due to negligence and Malachi, and Nyree would adopt him.

****

"So I want the Singapore Chow Mein, and Bruh Bruh wants Orange Chicken and… Daddy, are you even listening to me?" India asked.

"Yeah, yeah of course. You want what you always get at Wing Wah," Malachi responded not wanting to let India know that he really hadn't been listening as his mind drifted back down memory lane.

When Malachi arrived at Nyree's house, which the two of them affectionately referred to as the "Palace" with Chinese food and an extra combination platter, he was disappointed not to see her black Range Rover in the u-shaped heated driveway.

He and his children sat down at the dining room table and prepared to eat. *Where has the time gone? These kids look like young adults for real.* Malachi noticed that Christian was growing a full beard which was coming in nicely. Christian was nearly his height, six foot four and very athletic. It had been awhile since they had played a game of one-on-one. Malachi couldn't wait for spring to break so he could hoop his son and let him know that he still had skills on the court. He was blessed to have a beautiful daughter who was not trying to be fast. She was intelligent and dressed girly, but not sexy. They had raised her well. She was five foot eight and weighed one hundred fifteen pounds. India participated in the modeling troupe and had done some magazine and product promotions locally.

"Lord, we thank you for this food. Let it be used for the strength and nourishment of our bodies," he blessed the food because that is what Nyree would have required of him if she were home. Each place setting had a glass of water and a glass of Welch's grape juice. "Water then juice," he could hear her voice in his head saying. She was a stickler for consistency and organization.

"So, I'm guessing all homework has been completed?" Malachi asked.

"Geez, I thought Mom was bad, but I think you got her beat today. Like what's up with you, Dad?" India demanded.

Malachi laughed. He was just doing what any father would do. This is what he would do if he were in the household with them daily. There was a sense of guilt that flooded him. His children had never had him in the home consistently. Had he failed them? Had he cheated them? It was not all his fault as to why he hadn't been there, but his philandering had always been a problem, and he knew it. They would both be graduating in June, and he just wanted to be able to have some time with them. He wanted to be able to etch this moment into his memory. Neither one of his children were sure where they wanted to go to college. They didn't know if they would go to college right away after high school. Malachi knew this was the end of an era.

****

It dawned on him that he could have prevented this situation. His mind rewound to a time in the past when he sat at this very dining room table with Nyree.

Nyree had told him a few years ago, "Look you're a low budget type dude with no standards or morals. If I continue to deal with you what does that say about me? No need to answer. I'm not going to deal with it. It's too much stuff going on in the streets. Too much shit going around. Have you heard about this STD called BlueWaffles or BluePancakes? Anyways I'm not trying to be a victim of that. Don't look at me like I'm making this up. Google it if you don't believe me. Jumping in and out of beds, is that the life you want for yourself? You're sitting there thinking about it, go right ahead, but as for me, I'm done."

She had made it so plain. What could he say? In hindsight, there was a lot he could have said. He could have spoken from the heart and told her that she was wrong. It was the perfect opportunity to tell her he was not doing anything wrong, but his pride would not allow him to say anything. After all, when she made her mind up about something it was hard to undo that thought process. So, even though unjustly accused he didn't even try to speak up for himself or defend himself. He allowed her to think that he was a whoremonger. Eventually, he began to act out the things she said about him. Now, he was tired of the game. No woman ever did what Nyree did for him. This is the woman he wanted to settle down with for life.

****

"Dad, so are you going to just sit here and not answer our question?" Christian asked with an irritated tone.

Malachi was so wrapped up in his thoughts he hadn't even heard his son ask a question until now.

"Umm, I guess I just had a lot on my mind. It's been a long day so to speak," Malachi told them half-heartedly believing the words coming out of his mouth. "So, where is your mother? Did she say what time she'd be back? Her food is going to get cold."

"Dad, it's not like she knew you were coming by. Remember I asked you to bring the food by when you called. Like, get out your feelings."

He chuckled, "So, I'm in my feelings. I just don't want her food to get cold." Recently he heard that Nyree had been frequenting a jazz club with a younger guy who looked like he could be a model. He wondered if she was out with her young boyfriend. Malachi didn't know the rumor to be true, but there were becoming more and more evenings when she was not home, and so she very well could be out with someone.

"Yeah, okay. Like we're glad you're here and all, but we all know you're just trying to wait around so you can see Mom," Christian replied looking at the clock which indicated that it was six o'clock.

"Really, so that's what you think, Christian?"

"Nah. That's what I know, but it's cool. Why don't you call her and see what's keeping her? I will bet she's at the mall getting something for her birthday. You know it's Sunday. Hopefully, you got the perfect gift," Christian said.

"Dad, what's that look like I've got nothing as far as a gift is concerned?" India probed.

"Yeah, I hadn't thought about what I want to gift her with. Maybe you all can help me." *I can't win. I know when her birthday is, but it just came so quickly, and I'm not prepared. I don't know what I'm going to do this year. I bought my and her matching Range Rovers three years ago so I don't know what I can do to top that?*

After Malachi helped clean up the dining room and kitchen, he decided to leave but not before telling the children to have Nyree give him a call. As he left out the door, he called her cell phone which went to voice mail. He left a voice mail requesting that she gave him a call on tomorrow morning and reminded her that they had their weekly standing meeting, but they might need to make it a little later than normal. He had no real reason for suggesting it other than he hoped it would make her call him and ask why and then he could have a little bit of her time.

IVAN MARRICK

Ivan Marrick IV was wonderful to look at, and he knew it. He should have been a model. When he walked into a room, you had to take notice even if you didn't want to. He was six foot five, the color of creamy butter with sexy hazel eyes. A few times in his life he had been told that he looked like the actor slash model type. According to the females, he was Man Crush Monday for the females. . Ivan kept his hair cut low. He was in his barber's chair every Wednesday and Saturday. Every two weeks he had a mani-cure and pedicure. Everything was perfect about him. However he was a little self-conscious that his chest was flabby. He knew his chest wasn't flat, but one time when he was having sex with this woman who was riding his, she leaned in squeezed his pecs, lifted enough flesh to suck on and commented, "Your man titties are turning me on." While she had experienced multiple orgasms, he couldn't release himself. Her words haunted him. His waistline had a few unwanted inches as well.

He sat expressionlessly on the red micro suede couch in his beautiful three story home in Crown Point, Indiana listening to Rayna make excuse after excuse. *How long has this hoe been yapping off at the mouth?* Ivan found himself wondering. He had a high level of respect for women who deserved to be respected. His mother was a woman, so he respected women. At least that was the line he gave to women. Rayna didn't make his list.

His mind drifted to his mother as he listened to Rayna babble. He recalled once hearing his mother say that Rayna would be his downfall. *When 50 Cent, the rapper made that song "P.I.M.P." he was talking about me.*
"She like my style, she like my smile, she like the way I talk.
I ain't that nigga trying to holla cause I want some head.
I'm that nigga tryin' to holla cause I want some bread.
I could care less how she perform when she in the bed.
Bitch hit the track, catch a date, and come pay the kid."

Ivan and Rayna were a real live Bonnie and Clyde pair. They had been together on and off for the last ten years. He wouldn't call them a couple, but they were a couple. How could he call her his woman when she was out messing with another guy? He didn't trip on the fact that she was sleeping exclusively with Malachi Chandler. In fact, he made her want to sleep with Malachi. Ivan wanted her to be with him because it allowed him to live the lifestyle that he wanted. His eyes were fixed on the vaulted cathedral ceiling as she continued to tell him that Malachi was ending the relationship and for good this time.

Sucking his teeth, he sighed. "Okay, look, I hear you, Rayna, but you got to do something. How do you think we can live without him supplementing our income? I'm not the type of dude that is going to work a nine-to-five, and you know this." His head was pounding, and his heart was beginning to race.

Ivan grew up poor when he should have grown up privileged. His father; Ivan III had been an excellent businessman and owned a construction company in the City of Gary. The company did superb work. However, Ivan III had a drug habit that interfered with his performance. Sometimes the company would get jobs, and Ivan would have spent the money needed to purchase supplies on drugs. A few customers complained that items had come up missing when Marrick Construction workers were on site. Ivan III always found a way to speak with the customers and convince them not to press charges. He would say that he was trying to help rehabilitate some of the men on his crew, and he would handle the punishment internally. No one actually suspected it was Ivan III stealing.

"IV, stop sitting there staring into space. He just after two years dumped me at the winery. I never saw it coming."

"Rayna, come on. You did see it coming. It's just in times past we were able to dodge the bullet. Now you got to ask yourself what's different now? Why the finality? This is crazy, you had one task. Make him fall in love with you and get the money."

"I did that," she whined. "Honestly how long did you think it would last?"

"Rayna, stop talking okay. Your voice is irritating the hell out of me. I swear when it rains it pours. Today is just not my day. First I get a call from the nursing home saying that my mom is having difficulty breathing, now she's in ICU. Oh, did I tell you my dad went to visit her the other day, and the staff said that when they came back in to check on her that her radio and DVD player were gone? Really, and now I'm finding out that some of her jewelry is missing. Now you're telling me that you and Malachi are over. Yeah, this day just can't get any better." *I wonder if I can file a claim with the insurance company. The jewelry was on my policy. My damn daddy, I swear I hate him, and I've been cursed with his issues.*

****

Ivan allowed his mind to go to the past and think about when his father had been prosperous. At one point he had teamed up with the late Edwin Shaw, a prominent real estate businessman in the Midwest. Now his daughter, Nyree Shaw-Chandler was running the family business. Ivan III and Edwin were a dynamic team in the early 1980s. Ivan III had made an undisclosed amount of money and helped family members to get their piece of the American dream. Businesses for family members were established. Sisters, brothers, cousins, nieces, nephews were set up nicely and of course, his beloved wife, Charity, and son, Ivan IV, wanted for nothing.

Ivan III liked to relax by smoking marijuana and drinking with the fellows. Occasionally, he dibbled and dabbled with cocaine but always said he could handle it. Then in the 1980s when Ronald Reagan and George Bush were elected for a second term in office, something changed with Ivan III. He said the economy was changing, and there had been a problem with him and the IRS. All of a sudden, he owed them and hadn't been paying enough in taxes in previous years. "Always something to keep the Black man down," he would say. Ivan III then began to ease his sorrows more and more with cocaine and then when he was introduced to crack cocaine, life spiraled out of control. He had said the first high on crack was the equivalent of a female having her cherry popped. Every subsequent time he tried crack, he was looking to get that first-time mind blowing, vein popping orgasm. He said it never happened again, yet that never stopped him from chasing that high. He became instantaneously addicted.

If Ivan was not spending money to feed his crack habit, then he was feeding his gambling habit. Working and fulfilling jobs no longer mattered to Ivan III. The family lost their home in the early 1990s and Charity who never had to work a day in her life, now entered the workforce to provide for her and her son. She was smart and had some college education but didn't possess a degree. So while she was as capable as the next worker without the degree from an accredited university, she was unable to earn her worth. Charity used her feminine charm to compensate. At times she and Ivan III found themselves living with friends or in their car.

It grieved Ivan IV, he hated to see his mother struggle so he would steal things that women wanted and sell them at a lower rate. At an early age, he became a booster. He would go into upscale stores and shoplift designer bags and resell them to ladies for a lower price. When he got older, he had to increase his hustle to generate more revenue. Ivan liked going into jewelry stores and asking the store representative if he could view medium priced gold chains. He would ask to see some and then watch the representative put them back in the case. After a while, the store representative would become comfortable with him and forget to replace jewelry into the case. He would engage them in conversation and distract them by asking them to allow him to see more items and then slip items into his pocket.

Ivan had few regrets about his childhood exploits. There was one that ate away at his core. They didn't make enough drugs to erase the memory. His mother had a male friend named Johan Jamison. Ivan was made to call him Uncle J.J. Ivan never liked him. There was something very different about him. Uncle J.J.'s eyes seemed to linger too much on Ivan as opposed to his mother. Ivan could feel the heat from Uncle J.J.'s eyes on his penis. It made his uncomfortable. His mother told him, "Don't mess this up. We got a home now. We got a place to stay. I got money saved up for once, and we don't have to worry about where I next meal is going to come from. I know you don't like him, but please don't mess this up. For once in my life, I'm happy." Ivan had shaken his head to indicate he heard her, but he definitely didn't like it. His religious mother had as the church folk would say, "back slidden." But it did feel good not to have to be on the streets stealing.

One weekend, Uncle J.J. suggested that Charity go off with her friends and enjoy a weekend in downtown Chicago, and the boys would be fine at home. On Saturday night, Uncle J.J. had friends over to the house. It was a party much like the ones his dad used to have with marijuana and beer. He stayed in his room and then J.J. came in with another guy. "Hey Buddy," J.J. said, rubbing his hand on Ivan's thigh, a gesture he had never done before. Ivan flicked J.J.'s hand off his thigh. The other guy laughed. J.J. continued, "Look, this is my friend, Melvin. He wanna know if you want to make some money. He does not feel good, all you got to do is take care of him. Can you do that?" Melvin showed Ivan more hundred dollar bills than he had ever seen in his life. Ivan perked up. Rubbing his hands together, he inquired, "What I got to do?" J.J. smiled and left the room. Ivan still could feel the repetitive motion of Melvin's penis being shoved down his throat. He could still hear the moan that erupted from Melvin as he ejaculated into his mouth.

****

I've got to calm my nerves. Thinking about the dark days of his childhood always caused anxiety for him. He hated his mother for what happened to him, yet he loved her because she was his mother.

At thirty-eight years old he was finally beginning to come to grips with what happened to him as a child. It was not his mother's fault, but she should have had enough sense not to leave her nine-year-old child with a man she barely knew. His father should have been there to protect him. It was about that time for a little R&R. He walked over to the bar in his man cave. He retrieved his favorite drinking glass, rinsed it out with warm water and then poured Remy Martin Cognac Vintage 1989 in the eight -ounce glass.

Halfway filled, he stopped and then popped open a can of Red Bull and poured the contents into the glass. A few drops of grenadine to the concoction made it all the better. Sipping the R&R

made him feel slightly better, but he knew what was needed to cap off this experience. Opening the drawer to his desk, there was the prescription bottle with the yellow, happy pills. He immediately became happy just thinking about it. Xanax always made him feel happy. Now he could continue to endure Rayna's ranting about Malachi.

For a moment he was feeling homicidal.

"Ivan, look we've done well. This house is paid for. We have cars, and you have money that your businesses are generating. I just transferred two hundred thousand dollars to your account from Malachi's account, so what is the problem?"

She had a lot of nerve talking to him like that. He never talked to her about his expenses. Charity was living in that expensive facility, and he was paying cash. The cost of medical insurance when you are not employed is not a cheap thing. Rayna could be real naïve at times. *Did she just try to get self-righteous with me? Oh hell, naw. They had history. They went way back. They spent time together in the local group home.* He was the one that put her ragge-dy behind on to the game. Rayna had been living in Dorie Miller projects with her mother, her mother's boyfriend and six of her siblings. When she reconnected with Ivan she had been more than happy to commit scams, fraud, and now it sounded like she was talking about ending life as they knew it. No way.

Malachi Chandler was going to continue to supplement his lifestyle. Rayna didn't get it, but Ivan's vendetta with Malachi was personal. Malachi would never be able to right the wrong he had done, but he would pay. An eye for an eye and a tooth for a tooth.

He knew this day would come, and Rayna would make him hate her.

"Okay, Rayna, you're right. You know what, it is best that we probably lay low for a while. I will handle the bank account information like I always do, so he doesn't trace it back to you. Why don't you go back to the spot, pack up some things and maybe go out of town for a minute?" Ivan told her. The wheels in his head were spinning. He knew exactly what had to be done. He had the knowledge and resources to make it happen.

Rayna looked puzzled. "I don't know, Baby, are you sure? It's like one minute you're bitching about our lifestyle, and now you're saying we should go on vacation."

He cupped her face and looked into her big brown eyes. "It's okay, sweetheart, you've earned this vacation. I'm not going to be able to join you this time. Don't look like that. You know I love you right," he paused.

"Um, is this like a trick question? I always tell you I love you, and you just look like I ain't said a word. You always say you'll kill a bitch before you say you love her," Rayna asked looking into Ivan's green eyes.

Ivan was becoming infuriated by Rayna and quickly calmed himself. If he became too emotional, it would ruin what he had in store for Rayna. He kissed her passionately and then stroked her secret treasure with his fingers. This always diverted her attention from the issue. "You know I love you, Rayna, so just do what I ask, please," he softened his voice.

"Ivan, what will you do when I'm gone?" Rayna asked.

Laughingly he said, "I'm going to make sure everyone who has crossed us get's what they deserve. Now you deserve some relaxation. Call me when you get to the airport. You need to leave today."

"Ivan, what? You do know it's almost six o'clock. If I'm lucky to get a flight out it will be late tonight and you know I don't see well driving at night."

"Call me when you know what time your flight is going to leave and I will drive you to O'Hare or Midway. I got you taken care of. Never worry about little stuff like that sweetie."

"Thanks, baby, you're the best."

Pulling her into him, Ivan kissed Rayna deeply again. She returned the kiss and began caressing his body. He pulled away. "You got to go and book the flight, remember."

"Yes," Rayna tried to protest.

Ivan would not allow her to speak. Instead, he hurried her to the door and practically pushed her out. Rayna was seductive, and if she stayed any longer, they would have ended up in bed together. Ivan needed to focus, and the quickest way to get him off his game was for him to have sex. He had conditioned himself to not feel anything for Rayna lately.

The only thing he felt towards her was hate. He believed, at his core, he had always hated her. The feeling had intensified about two months ago on January 1, 2016.

****

The conversation replayed in his head. "What do you mean my mother is the biggest problem I have in my life? My mother is dying, and that's what you propose to say to me?"

"Before she got diagnosed with cancer she was your biggest problem. You can choose to ignore it if you want to or deal with it. She's the reason you were in and out of juvenile detention centers and group homes. If she had been a better mother to you and not let you do whatever you wanted to do... never mind because you place her on this high pedestal, but deep down you harbor resentment towards her." Ivan had refused to address Rayna's comments about his mother. He hated her for speaking so freely. Ivan talked a lot, but he could never articulate his feelings about his mother. That was a weak spot for him. It felt as if Rayna had reopened a wound that never completely healed. What a way to start the New Year!

****

As he brought himself back in the moment, he was beginning to think that 2016was not his year. He remembered the days of going to church and hearing the preacher quote Proverbs 29:25, "The fear of man will prove to be a snare." The day he had dreaded was here---his gravy train had derailed, and Rayna was partially to blame. Now he had to take matters into his own hands. At thirty-eight years old he had acquired and blown a substantial amount of wealth. He looked good on paper, and he planned to continue to live the lifestyle he had grown accustomed to living. Malachi Chandler had been his meal ticket, and he just was not quite ready to say, "Sayōnara."

He was not going to stress himself out. His plan was to get into bed and relax. Tomorrow would be a new day, and he was going to go to Chaotic Bliss Day Spa and get a massage. His hope was to bump into Malachi Chandler.

MALACHI CHANDLER

Malachi bolted up in his king sized bed. Struggling to get his feet untangled in the sheets was not proving to be an easy task. This would not even have been a problem if he had a bed partner. "What in the hell is going on?" *I know good and damn well, ain't nobody trying to break in here.* Malachi thought as he heard pounding on windows and doors as he lay in bed. He propped himself up on his pillows in the bed and looked at the video camera footage of his home on his cell phone. Squinting at the image of the woman at his front door he questioned if it were Rayna. *Yep, she's pissed that her key no longer works. Did she think she would continue to have access to my house? Rayna can't be that stupid. I always did think she was a bit naïve. She's embarrassing herself. I don't need any more bad press, I really don't.*

Why is it that when I break up with females, they never take it well? Aris was the same way when I cut ties with her. I just want to be with one woman---Nyree. It's taken me twenty years to come to this epiphany, but I know what I want, and I'm going to have what I want. I just hope now that I know what I want, it's not too late. Hopefully, this young guy she is ripping and running the streets with hasn't sold her a pie in the sky dream. I love Nyree, but she doesn't always have a level head when it comes to guys. Colin Jordan damned near had her believing that he was an angel walking the earth. You couldn't say nothing bad about Saint Colin. He first fell from grace when India was at death's door as an infant. Colin was playing daddy to my daughter, but when I came around he knew to blend into the background, and he couldn't take it. This clown had a melt-down, accused me and Nyree of having sexual relations in my daughter's hospital room. Nyree cursed him out in English, Spanish, and some other tongue. His final fall from grace was when he tried to kill me at Nyree's father's burial. I don't know what possessed Nyree to step in front of that gun toting fool. Ride or die chick, that's Nyree for real. She took a bullet to the shoulder for me. I will forever love that woman.

Malachi rushed downstairs to open the door to speak to Rayna. He was wearing only his Ralph Lauren pajama bottoms when he opened the door. Seemed like a good idea while he was in bed, but that bitter cold air sent a chill through his body.

Shivering as he braced his bare upper body by folding his arms across his chest, Malachi gave Rayna a piercing look. "You do know it is seven o'clock and whatever you thought you needed to say could have been said via text or phone. Why are you here?" he asked through a cracked door.

"So, you're going to make me stand out here. You're not going to let me in? What, you got company?"

"Nope. I just don't want you in my house. You're a raving lunatic," he told her as she pushed her way into the house.

"I'm not leaving until I have some answers. I need closure and you me owe that," Rayna told him.

"You know what, you might be right, and if I respected you as a woman or even as a person, I might give you that. However, since I don't respect you, I won't give you that courtesy."

The look on her face told Malachi that Rayna was flabbergasted. His response was definitely one she hadn't anticipated.

"You know what Rayna, I will tell you this much. Something about you lately has been off. I mean your aura has not been right. I couldn't quite put my finger on it until I received a call from my accountant about a money trail at the station. It seems you have been taking money and investing it in a record label. I mean… and that's cool and all, but what else are you lying about? I don't trust you. And then you started trying too hard to befriend my children. Like on New Year's Eve when Christian got into that accident, and you just so happened to be in the area to be able to assist him. Yeah…," he said and began shaking his finger as if things were becoming crystal clear to him. He continued, "Yeah, your whole excuse about not feeling well and having to leave the party we were hosting. Umph, yeah, that lame excuse never did add up and then…then you just so happen to be there to help my son out. I could be paranoid, or I could be dead-ass right, which one is it?"

"How about you are paranoid? You're dead ass wrong. A record label investment and Christian's accident, which I totally had nothing to do with is your grounds for breaking up with me. You know what, you need to stop smoking weed. I think somebody might have given you some of that "Ooo No." You're tripping hard."

"Ha, ha. You're funny. That shows how much you're in tune with me. I haven't smoked in about a year or so. And that's another thing you do…instead of owning up to your mess ups, you try to divert the attention away from you and point the blame on others. It doesn't even matter, I'm ridding myself of all trash, including you," he said as he ushered her out the door.

She turned around and looked him in the eye and said, "Fuck you, Malachi."

He laughed in her face and said, "No thank you, already done that."

His quick responses had a way of eating at her core. Unable to respond with a snappy reply, she smacked his face, rushed past him out of the door and hopped into her black BMW.

"Get out of here and drive off to Thotland," he snickered as he slammed the door. Although he laughed, the situation was not funny. Rayna had thoroughly pissed him off.

Running up the stairs to his bedroom, he stood at the side of the bed shaking. There was something about that woman that made him want to hit her. He was not even the type of guy who would hit a female, but Rayna had him raging. Yesterday she had thrown wine on him at the winery and today she had literally slapped the taste out of his mouth. When she smacked him, he had drooled. Rayna was not a bad person. She really was not, other than the money issue that had come up recently. Deep down in his heart he thought there was a good reason for her taking the money and sending it to this business account called Musically Inclined.

Malachi remembered how desperate he had been in his twenties. He had stolen from Nyree and his baby's mother, whom it hurt him to say her name so he just referred to the woman as "Her." Desperation will make you do some unethical things he recalled. However, Rayna was sitting in a pretty economic bracket so why was she stealing? He couldn't let that go. Even though he had been afforded grace and mercy for his deeds in the past, extending it to Rayna was difficult. The thought of filing a police report was running through his mind as well. Malachi was feeling vengeance in his heart. Rayna should pay for what she did, he found himself thinking. He paced the floor so much at the foot of his bed until he thought he would wear a hole in the plush black carpet. It had been a year since he smoked marijuana but right now would be the perfect time to roll a blunt if he had some weed on hand. A drink would be nice. *I am not going to let her drive me to drinking.*

Walking into his closet, he wondered what he would wear today. He looked at the reflection of himself in the mirror and decided that his stomach looked good. Anger overcame him, and he pounded on the mirror with his fist and watched glass shards fly past him as small pieces kissed his shoulders and feet. Dusting himself off he walked over to his Jordan collection and picked up shoes Rayna had purchased and thrown them at the mirror. Walking out of the closet without cleaning the mess up, he promised himself he would just get another hour of sleep before he went to his office.

Jumping back into bed, he thought about the kid's birthday party he was going to perform at on Friday. What songs would he perform? Finally, he exhaled and told himself to let tomorrow take care of tomorrow. Right now there was more sleep to be had, and he was a willing participant.

NYREE CHANDLER

Nyree's face felt numb. She could barely feel her finger's. She sniffed a little as the weather caused her nose to feel as though it were getting ready to run. Shivering uncontrollably as she removed her snow boots at the front door of her home. Her feet were tingling. "Girl, what are you doing? All that noise?" Nicole Rouse- Shaw asked Nyree.

Nyree laughed into the blue tooth. Her best friend was very observant, she didn't miss a beat. Nyree supposed that was what made Nicole such an excellent attorney. Nyree hadn't realized the blue tooth picked up that well. "Girl," she laughed, "you so nosey. Oh my gosh, I guess that's why you're one of the best attorneys in the Midwest. I'm over here trying not to get the floor wet with these boots. Girl, that temperature has dropped. I can barely feel my feet," Nyree told her as she hobbled around in the foyer trying to be careful not to let her feet step on the mat where snow quickly turned into water.

"Honey, where are you coming from? Kyle and I said if we didn't have to be out, we wouldn't be out. This snow is coming down so fast. We almost thought we weren't going to be able to get a flight out of Orlando. They were talking about the bad weather that was going to hit the Chicagoland area."

"I just got in from having a massage. I needed it." Nyree sighed.

"Umph, I bet," Nicole said with a bit of sarcasm. Going into full lawyer mode, she continued, "And did you see Malachi? I know you all are going to be doing something for your birthday. Sunday will be here before you know it. I sure hope you are not snowed in for it."

"No, I didn't see Malachi. I went to his office, but he wasn't in there. Strange because we are supposed to have our meeting today. He left me a message last night and said it would have to be later than we usually have it, but I haven't heard from him. That's weird because usually when we have it later, he will say something like 'I'm going to Chicago and probably won't make it back in time.' I don't know. You don't think he went over to Chicago and experienced some trouble, do you? Girl, they are killing people left and right in Chicago. Even in upscale neighborhoods. Those smash and grabs are becoming more common place. Girl, I'm rambling. He probably had a late night out with that tramp."

"Okay, Nyree. So, tell me how you really feel. Now, I'm guessing you didn't suddenly need a massage," Nicole teased Nyree, "y'all are so funny. I wish you all would just keep it real and go ahead and be with each other."

"Whatever Nikki, you know he's with that old ratchet chick, Rayna. Anyway, I'm still cold from being outside. It's arctic cold out there. Why did I let Malachi convince me to purchase a home on the lakefront?"

"Oooh, oooh, me, I got the answer," Nicole stated, sounding like a kid in an elementary classroom. Not waiting for a response from Nyree, she followed up her statement with, "Ten years ago, you all thought it was a great idea. You guys were going to work on you all and be a family. Kyle and I are really rooting for you all. I think deep down in your heart you know he is your guy."

"I used to think that. I will be forty-five on Sunday, and I don't know. I don't know if I want to waste any more good years on what could be, or what if. I think it's time to live and live now. You know for over the last ten years I have lived in fear. You remember how Colin in a jealous rage shot up my dad's burial ceremony. I got hit with that bullet and even though I didn't die, a part of me died. There I was like I was some real gangster type chick stepping in front of a gun-toting man to protect Malachi. I know Colin was angry and jealous and trying to get me back, but that was crazy. I still don't like being out in open spaces. I'm rambling, but oh let me tell you this. How about you will never guess who was at the spa…"

"Who? Who, Girl?"

"Ivan Marrick's fine self. He asked me for my number again. He said he got a new phone and for some reason, all of the numbers didn't transfer over. I told him if he wants to talk to me he will find a way to get it."

"Nyree, what about Malachi? And didn't you go out with him a couple of times and say that something was kind of off about him. He was always bragging about his political connections and his money. Like you weren't feeling him."

"Nikki, have you been listening? It's time for me to have some fun and do me. I think I kept trying to compare him to Malachi. Like I wanted him to be a better version of Malachi. I didn't give him a fair chance because I kept trying to make him into somebody he will never be." *Nyree shocked herself with her analysis of the situation.*

"2016, just might be the year that Nyree gets her groove back." They both laughed.

"I know y'all not on that phone cackling and laughing about me," Nyree heard her brother, Kyle Shaw say to Nikki.

"Girl, tell Kyle everything in life is not about him. And don't mention what I told you. You know he will have something to say. Look, I know you all probably got jet lag. Thanks for calling me and letting me know you all made it back safely. I am going to sit on this couch and get caught up on my missed episodes of Empire and Power. Girl, you know who else is a fine brother, 50 Cent. Oh my goodness I bet he got the magic stick for real."

"Oh my," Nikki gasped, "I wasn't ready for that," she said trying to imitate comedian, Kevin Hart. Nyree laughed, and Nikki continued, "You and your shows, I tell you."

"Yes, Missy, it is what keeps me sane in an insane world and with these teenagers, oh my goodness."

"Yes, Mama Margo, told me the kids are staying with her for a while so you really got time to get your groove back with Ivan Marrick."

"Dang, you can't keep nothing. I said don't let Kyle get wind of it. You know he likes to ear hustle," Nyree said.

"Okay, I won't say anything else about it. I'm in the family room, and I think he's in the kitchen. Girl, Kyle is off in his own little world. You know he thinks he's Chef Boyardee. We watched some cooking show, and Kyle said as soon as we got home he was going to make that dish," Nikki told her, "well honey all I can say is, be happy. And some hot amazing birthday sex. Be happy and have great sex in that order." Nikki believed everyone should be as happy as she and her husband and always told people to do what made them happy.

"Girl, bye," Nyree said as she tried to think about the last time she had some hot amazing sex. The closest she had come to a romantic encounter would have been two months ago. She had shared a long passionate kiss with Malachi after coming from one of the comedy shows at Hustle & Joe's Club. Malachi had walked her to the door and made sure she had gotten into the house. Generally, after she unlocked the door, he would tell her to hurry and lock the door and then walk back to his vehicle. This particular night, he followed her in. When she turned to look him in the eye and question what he was doing, he drew her in closely and kissed her. She returned the kiss. Before any words could be exchanged, he told her to lock up and that he would text her and let her know he had made it home safely.

As she eased into her chair in front of her computer to check her email, her mind drifted to the encounter she had with Ivan at the Chaotic Bliss Spa. She didn't know what she wanted in life. Here she was creeping up on forty-five years old, and she still didn't know what she wanted out of life. *Damn shame,* she told herself. Yes, she had degrees, certifications, money in the bank and a cold, king size bed. She loved her wonderful children, but they were nearly grown. Christian and India would be graduating in a few months, and although they both had many options on the table for life after high school, nothing was set in stone. Nyree knew most people would do the "Running Man" just thinking how close they were to being an empty nester. She cringed. The thought of being alone in her home was not a comfortable feeling.

A hurtful thought gnawed at her as well. What if Christian decided when he graduated that he wanted to go be with his biological mother? They had many conversations and Christian always said that he didn't want to visit his biological mother because she never showed up for the visitations. Nyree was always careful to assure him that if he wanted a relationship with his biological mother that would not hurt her feelings and he should pursue it. Christian was a well-mannered and quiet child, but when he wanted something he went after it wholeheartedly. Nyree loved Christian and spent most of his life assuring him that she loved him. Guilt, still worked her over as she nearly killed him with her reckless driving.

For the past twenty plus years, she and Malachi had been on and off. There was the thought that this time, it could really work, but how many times had she fed herself that lie.

Dismissing the thought of Malachi, she allowed herself to re-focus on her original thought---Ivan Marrick. His name sounded like a character off of a soap opera. That was a fine specimen of a man if ever she had seen one. He was fair skinned with green eyes. Some women in the race were "color struck"- meaning they didn't date darker skinned males. Nyree was the complete opposite. She liked her ice-cream in a multitude of flavors. He was the total opposite of her ex-husband who was also a fine specimen that was a charcoal complexion.

A smile graced her face as she remembered how Ivan had flirted with her in the waiting area by the fireplace. "You seem way too relaxed to need a massage?" The words rolled smoothly off his tongue as she sipped her hot chocolate.

Nyree recalled having turned and looked at him. Her eyes had been drawn to his perfect lips. For a moment, she imagined those lips gently coming into contact with her own lips. "I had an amazing massage earlier. I always like to sit in the waiting area after my treatment and sip tea before I go home. Today, however, I needed hot chocolate," she found herself explaining as she sat fully clothed in the chair next to him. The warmth of the fireplace felt nice. He seemed completely comfortable sitting next to her in the leather reclining chair wearing nothing but a black terry cloth robe with CB monogrammed on the right side and IV over his heart. Nyree couldn't help but wonder if he was wearing underwear underneath his robe. She knew for a fact that Malachi wore underwear when he was getting massaged. Ivan didn't seem like the type who would wear underwear. She had nothing to base her conclusion on because she barely knew the guy; it was just something she had made up about him in her mind. Her eyes continued to scan him and check him out. He was wearing UGG Ascot slippers furnished by the spa to keep his feet warm. He must be a regular because only regulars have their names on their robes. It was odd because she never remembered seeing him at the spa. Malachi had never mentioned him either. While the spa was Malachi's venture, he often consulted with her and picked her brain about ways to improve the spa. He often joked, "I am going to make you put that expensive degree from Indiana University to work here at Chaotic Bliss."

Something about Ivan's status at the spa didn't seem right. Nyree recalled that her father had worked on ventures with Ivan Marrick III in the past. She did know much about the Marrick family other than they were well off. There was a son she had heard about that was down south doing something with the music industry. This had to be the same young man she had heard about in gossip columns. Even though, she and Ivan had gone out a couple of times for coffee and lunch she didn't know much about him. When she thought about it, she knew more of what the rumor mill said about him than his actual mouth had told her. Shameful, she knew it; she hated being the topic of gossip but loved reading it when it pertained to others. This gentleman was very handsome, and she felt his eyes on her. Perhaps she was staring at him, and that is why he was staring at her. She made a mental note to ask Malachi about him when she talked to him later.

Setting her coffee mug on the coaster on the coffee table, she scooted to the edge of the seat and lifted her behind off of her chair. At her age, her muscles and bones became stiff when she sat for long periods of time. Sometimes she would stand up, and pain would radiate through her body, and she would be stiff as a board. This calculated movement got the muscles to moving before she really needed them and then she would not experience pain when she stood up. "Well, enjoy your massage," she told him and stretched a little.

"I plan to do so. Hey, I know this may sound crazy, but do you think I could buy you a hot chocolate one day?"

"Umm…" Nyree giggled. *Really did I just giggle like some teenage girl? What the hell is wrong with me?*

"Mom, Mom" India and Christian barged into the waiting area, "we are so happy to have caught up with you," India said. She was always doing all the talking and Christian would just nod his head occasionally to signal that he was on board with what his sister was saying.

"Okay, so let me understand why you two are not in school at this time of the morning."

Christian cleared his throat and announced, "Mamaja, have you not seen the news? There is like a blizzard coming this way. It's three inches of snow on the ground, and the snow that's falling is as big as cotton balls. Anyways, Grandmaja says we can stay the rest of the week with her until after your birthday."

Nyree said, "Okay so you all know that today is only Wednesday, right? My birthday isn't until Sunday. And let me get this straight, my mother, Margo, said you all can stay with her all that time? Hell must have just frozen over."

"Yep and yep. Wait until you go out there and feel how cold it is, "Christian said happily with a laugh.

"Well, if you're going you guys need to get in Christian's truck and get there, especially if the weather is anything like you said." Nyree began putting on her leather coat. Her bulky sweater made it a little difficult to ease her arms into her sleeves. Ivan jumped up and immediately assisted her. She inhaled his cologne and found it to be quite captivating.

"So about the hot cocoa, did you answer me?"

"Persistent. Umm, I guess that would be okay but I..."

"What? You're trying to think of an excuse to turn me down, but you can't think of anything," he laughed.

She nodded her head. Smiling she told him, "I can think of a lot of things to say, but maybe we can just clean the slate between us and have a fresh start. You apparently recognize an amazing woman when you encounter one." What made her say all of that she had no answer? She was having fun with the conversation. They had gone out a couple of times for lunch. Nothing ever really became of it. The last time they were supposed to go out the timing just seemed to be off and after that, they lost contact with one another. That had been during the holiday season. Her children even looked at her curiously.

"So Mamaja, you're just going to cake in front of us?" Christian wanted to know. Nyree tried to go to her slang repertoire of words to decipher "cake." She concluded that it must have something to do with flirting. Laughing off the comment she said, "Call me when you all make it to your grandmother's house," Nyree told her children and then turned her attention to Ivan, "I guess I will speak with you later, Mr. Marrick."

"How will I do that without a number?"

Nyree frowned. " Oh, so you unprogrammed my phone number," she scrolled through her phone and said, "yep, I still have you locked into my phone. Wow," she said pretending to have hurt feelings.

"See, here you go. No, it's not like that. I dropped my phone outside one night, and as luck would have it, I ran over it. Long story short, I didn't have all my numbers backed up to Google and lost a lot of contacts. Don't be like that, sweetheart, let me get your number."

"Nope. We're going to see how serious you are about wanting to talk to me. I've always taken you for a resourceful guy, I'm sure you will get **it** if you want **it**." She walked out of the sitting area.

****

There was nothing of interest in her email. She decided to relax her mind and made her way to her leather sofa, curled up with a blanket and turned on the television, scrolled to recorded items and clicked on the screen to watch this week's past episode of Empire.

Her phone notification indicated she had a text message. It was from a number that was not programmed and it simply said, "Hello Beautiful, hope you're staying warm." She smiled at the message. It had to be Ivan. Was he trying to see if he could get

49

invited over to keep her warm? Clever guy, she thought because it was frigid cold in Gary, Indiana, but he would have to lay more charm on than that. She'd be lying if she said the thought of his muscular arms around her body hadn't popped up more than once in her mind. There were a lot of things she had been delivered from in her life. Her grandmother had prayed for her and laid hands on her with the blessed oil. However, men were and continued to be her weakness. Nyree struggled with lust. Now that is not to say she acted out all her lustful fantasies, but she knew she should not even be entertaining that thought with this guy.

She returned his text and said, "Yes, I am staying warm."

"I'd like to buy you some hot chocolate. Can I do that tonight along with dinner?"

Nyree found herself looking at her phone and thinking, he doesn't waste any time getting to the point. She peeped out the window and saw the snow coming down heavily. There were weather alerts coming across her phone suggesting that motorist avoids being out on the roads if they didn't have to be on the roads. The school district had canceled school for the next day, and it was suggested school would probably be canceled on Friday as well. She sat her phone down and decided not to respond promptly.

The phone rang as she settled back onto the sofa. "Hey Beautiful," the smooth voice bolted.

"Hi," Nyree said giddily.

"So, I thought we could have dinner at T.J. Maloney's in the Radisson."

"Whoa, let me get this straight, you want to take me to a hotel on our first date?"

He laughed, "Technically it's not a first date. To answer your question, nah, I want to take you to dinner on our first official date. You want to make me sound like a bad guy and say I want to take you to a hotel on our first date. Sweetie, look I ain't gonna lie to you. I like pussy so if you want to give me some on our quote unquote first date, I'm not going to turn it down, but I don't think you're that type. You're the type that a brother has to prove himself to and work hard to get it. And I don't mind working to gain your love and trust but again if you want to give it to me on the first date since we are starting over."

Nyree found herself shaking her head. She hadn't expected him to be that blunt. "Umm…I don't give up my goods that easily, Ivan. The weather is bad, so I am going to have to decline your dinner invitation."

"The plows have been out. Come on and have dinner with me."

"I would love to, but I don't have a driver tonight, and I don't drive when it's bad."

"What? Are you serious? You don't have a driver so you won't have dinner with me? Like you really can't drive yourself to the restaurant. Damn, you really are full of yourself."

Taken aback, Nyree said, "You really don't know me. You may have heard and read about me, but you don't know anything about me. I don't give a doggone what the papers say or what you've read. I don't drive when it's bad outside. Yes, I have a driver. Not because I have money, but because when my son was little, I nearly killed him because I didn't see him in the street and I was driving reckless. So, excuse me for being traumatized by that and thinking of others safety and not wanting to drive in adverse conditions. You know what? I don't owe you an explanation. Enjoy your dinner," and she hung up on him. The nerve of that bastard to suggest she was acting siditty.

The phone rang several times, and she allowed it to go to voicemail. It was Ivan. He had thoroughly pissed her off. The phone rang again and continued to ring. It was him again. He was not going to be put off that easily.

"What?" Nyree answered.

"Sweetie, did you just hang up on me?"

"Yes, I did. I don't have anything else to say."

"Nyree, you don't think that you're being a bit childish."

"You know what Ivan, I don't have anything to say to you." She began doubting if she would ever meet a suitable suitor. Maybe she was just destined to be old and lonely.

"I wanted to apologize for being presumptuous…"

"Okay, can I call you back in a moment? Someone is at the door," she rushed him off the phone without waiting for him to respond.

IVAN MARRICK

After being rushed off the phone by Nyree, Ivan sulked, feeling dejected. He eased his pain by devouring most of his ten piece wing meal from Gowdy's. There were one and a half wings left with a few French fries remaining in the sauce saturated container. He was feeling sluggish from lack of rest and decided to leave the container on top of the wrinkled brown paper bag on his night-stand. Ordinarily, he didn't eat or drink in his bedroom, but today he was making an exception. His body convinced him that he needed to lie down for some much-needed rest.

The call he received from Nick, his mother's nurse had left him feeling uneasy. "Ivan, we waited for you as long as we could before we transported Charity to have her biopsy. What happened? That's not like you to miss an appointment and something as serious as this," Nick inquired.

Ivan had completely forgotten. The feeling of inadequacies he had felt as a child swept in after Nick's slight reprimand. Rayna usually reminded him about things like that and coordinated his schedule. "A last minute business crisis came up that required me to handle it," Ivan lied.

"Oh," Nick said not sounding convinced, "well, we got the results back, and it looks like the cancer is back. Tumors were found in her larynx. The prognosis is not looking good. We haven't shared the results with her yet. Do you want us to wait until you're here or tell her?"

"Nick, we can wait until tomorrow or the day after," Ivan suggested. He knew he was not going to make it to the hospital today. Letting out a sigh he asked, "How is she doing otherwise?"

Ivan was always aware that his mother was in a fight for her life. Hearing Nick's words just made him think that she might not win the battle.

"Charity is resting well and seems to be as comfortable as her condition will allow her to be," Nick reported. A couple of months ago she had lost her mobility, and it upset her. Her voice had become raspy, and she constantly complained of her throat hurting. The results of the biopsy now spoke to what was going on with her voice. He wanted to go see her, but he was exhausted.

The majority of his days and nights were with her at the private nursing home. It cost him nearly five thousand dollars per month to house her there. The update from Nick added to his worry and anxiety. Ivan decided to close his eyes to get some rest from reality. He dreamed that he was having dinner with Nyree Chandler. She looked so angelic and was in the middle of saying, "I want you so..." and as luck would have it his phone rang and interrupted the dream.

Ivan bolted up in his bed. Whenever his phone rang, he never knew if it would be the dreaded call that his mother passed away. Onyx Green and the nursing home had the same ring tone. He kept telling himself that he would change the ringtones but never got around to doing so. Ivan let out a sigh when he saw Onyx's name flash across the screen. "Yeah, what's up Onyx? Did she make it to the airport?" Ivan inquired as he rubbed his eyes.

"No, she's still in Gary. Now, you said she told you that she purchased her ticket, she's lying. I was able to get into her computer and phone, and she hasn't even searched for a ticket. Your girl is playing a game with you."

"It would seem that she is playing a game that she incapable of winning. That's okay. I will let her play a little while longer. So, since she's still in Gary what has she been doing?" Ivan asked as he began nibbling on the remains of his food. He was a bit irritated that this matter hadn't gone as planned, but he would not allow himself to speak negative thoughts on the situation.

****

Ivan recalled sitting across from his mother at the Beach Café last summer. As she sat across from him looking in her compact, he recalled her smiling at her reflection. Sixty years old and she still had men in their thirties turning their heads. His mother always prided herself on looking well. As she dabbed her thin lips with a hint of lip gloss and smoothing her hair back, she commented, "Son, I'm telling you, Rayna, that's one no good heifer. Now, I like her as a person, but not for my son. That woman is going to be your downfall. Just as sure as it is day right now, she is going to be the death of you."

"Ah, Ma, ain't nobody trying to hear that prophetic stuff. Ain't nobody going to be the death of me. Do you know how many times I've escaped death, Ma? Remember when we were left for dead in that underground cave? Did we die, nope? Do you know how many bullets I've dodged?"

"That's just it, Ivan, there's going to come a day you are going to face a bullet you can't dodge. That day comes for us all. Speaking of which, Baby," she began to cry.

"Damn, Ma, what is it? Don't be out here crying. These people looking at me like I'm upsetting you, here take this napkin," he handed her a napkin. When the tears continued to flow from his mother's eyes, he started rocking back and forth. That was a soothing technique one of his therapists had suggested to him when he was in juvenile detention facilities as a child.

Shaking his head and inhaling air from deep within his belly and exhaling through his nose, he closed his eyes, "Ma, what is it?"

Her voice cracked, "I met with Dr. Octavius yesterday..."

Ivan squinted, "The oncologist? What did you do that for?"

"I had my wellness check last week and... damn, the cancer is back. I'm not doing chemo, this time, Ivan."

The waitress walked past, and Ivan yelled, "Excuse me, Sweetheart, can we get the check please?"

"Sure," the waitress scooted off.

"Did you hear me, Ivan, no chemo this time," Charity said. Her features mirrored her sons. Her hazel eyes were focused on him, but he would not look her in her eyes.

"Ma, I'm not trying to hear that. We tried that all natural, vegan, healthy gross looking juices and we are going to do whatever it takes. Who gonna cook my greens and cornbread on Sunday? Gigi already up in heaven cooking for the saints. And now you trying to tell me you ain't going to be around? Nope. We're going to fight this out. You came back from this before. You did it once, you'll do it again.'

Charity smacked her son on the hand and laughed. "Yes, child. I've been kicking ass and taking names my whole life. I'm tired."

"Ma, I'm really not trying to hear that. You got to be here to cook my greens and cornbread on Sunday's," he told her trying to make light of the situation. He knew it was serious, but he just was not ready to deal with the reality of it. He had lost his grandmother four years ago and just was not ready to deal with another loss. He knew it was the cycle of life, but could it just bypass him and move on to someone else.

Charity smiled and smacked her son on the hand, "Umph, you better come get you some cooking lessons. These young broads out her nowadays can barely work a microwave. They barely know their cooch from a hole in the wall," she told him stealing her last line from the movie, "Poetic Justice."

They both laughed. Charity's mood became serious as she smacked Ivan on the hand again, "Remember what I said about Rayna."

****

It made sense to him now. As he thought about it, that statement was one of the last things he remembered her saying before the dreadful disease took her ability to speak. Ivan had taken it as a cliché statement until last night. Rayna wanted to know why he was not interested in her sexually. "Because you're a hoe," he told her matter of factly. When the words came out of his mouth, he felt a tinge of regret, but his pride would not allow him to apologize. It was a true statement that he should not have spoken. Rayna was feisty, but her response was one he had never expected. She huffed. Carefully enunciating every word she said, "So, I'm a hoe?"

"Yes Rayna, you're a whore," Ivan told her calmly. He didn't like reminiscing much, but it was necessary to drive his point home. "Remember when you were screwing every dude who said, 'hi' to you and you thought you were pregnant. Remember when you slipped a pregnancy test into your pants while in Walgreens and used their bathroom to get your results immediately. Yeah, I think that actually over qualifies you for being a whore."

Rayna shook her head in disbelief, "Hmm, what does that make your momma?"

Ivan recalled rubbing his eyes as if that would impact his hearing. He didn't have a retort. "Huh?" he questioned because clearly, Rayna hadn't implied that his mother was anything than the queen on the pedestal he had placed her on.

"Huh, I know you heard what I said," Rayna responded.

"Leave my mother out of this. She has nothing to do with this. You're mad because I don't want you ass, how could I after everything that's been through you? You forget I remember your humble beginnings."

Rayna tossed her head and laughed, "Oh my, you forget I remember your beginnings or maybe I should school you on your beginnings. I remember you from the group home, and you remember me from the group home too. You were in the group home sucking dick for money. It probably felt natural to you, after all; your momma was pimping you out to men and whomever. She had you out there stealing for her and to bring in money by any means necessary. We both had some crappy childhoods, and we were there for each other, but your childhood was worse than mine. Your momma was out there sleeping with every Tom, Dick, and Harry. Hoe, I believe I misspoke, she's worse than a whore. Look in the mirror. Have you ever wondered why you don't look like your daddy? Maybe that's because he ain't your daddy. Your daddy is a white man and Ivan III loved your momma so much that he gave you his name and to deal with his shame and misery he gets high."

****

"She's been quite busy. I spotted her at Malachi Chandler's house this morning. He wouldn't let her in. From what I could see it appears that she was arguing with him. She hit him a couple of times, and he just stood there and took it. He said something and then slammed the door in her face. Then about an hour ago she went over to Nyree Chandler's house. Now apparently Nyree doesn't have as much patience as her ex because..." Onyx hesitated.

"Because what?" Ivan asked as he munched on his food. Smacking his lips he continued, "You can't start telling a story and then act like you want to hold out. Because what?" Ivan asked impatiently as he licked the sauce from his fingers. His attention had been piqued. Perhaps it was Rayna who was at the door and whom she had rushed him off the phone to deal with.

"I didn't want to be spotted, but Nyree looked like she had a gun in her hand as she pushed Rayna out the door."

After a few seconds of coughing uncontrollably, "Damn Onyx, you almost made me choke on this chicken wing. I'm eating some of this fire chicken from Gowdy's. You say," he paused swallowing as he still had a tickling sensation in his throat, "chick had a gun at Rayna's head? Nyree doesn't seem like the type to be gun toting."

Onyx replied, "IV, what are you basing this on, what you've read or seen on television? I bet chick is not as sweet and innocent as she comes off as being. This is a business woman who's amassed great wealth. You know she couldn't have done that by being America's Sweetheart? She may have you Gary folks fooled, but not me. I've traveled across the world. I've worked in high and low places. I'm a paid killer. I served in Desert Storm and dealt with the enemy, not saying she's an enemy, but I know a lot about human behavior. Get caught in a tight situation and you'll start doing and saying stuff you'd thought you would never do. It's my job to watch, observe, and know people and while she's not my focus. I know her public persona is not her true persona."

Ivan laughed. Onyx was always going to give you solid information with a monologue. There was always a conspiracy theory associated with the things he said. Ivan was waiting for Onyx to say that Nyree had sold her soul to the Illuminati, and that is how she became wealthy. Next, he would say that her father had been sacrificed so that the family could continue to operate and pass wealth to the next generation. Onyx would soon say that there was no way that this operation could be run by African Americans in Gary, Indiana which was an impoverished community unless the government allowed it. Onyx often said the reason why Ivan's family business hadn't flourished like the Shaw's family business had nothing to do with skill set.

According to Onyx, it had everything to do with Ivan Marrick III. When Ivan III would not sell out and play the game, he was taken out the game. Not killed, but put in a position where he could no longer play. His mind was altered by drugs, so even if he wanted to let people know what was going on, who would listen to him. No one was going to believe the ramblings of a crack head. So, while he wasn't killed physically, he was killed. To live daily in a state of knowing what you once had, but now without any means of achieving it had to be a death that Ivan died daily. Often Ivan wondered about his dad. Could Onyx be right about him? It didn't really matter because Ivan harbored so much anger and hate toward him.

Onyx had served in the United States Army during Operation Desert Storm. After successfully serving twenty years in the Army he retired. Now he was back home in Gary trying to rid the streets of toxins and toxic people. Ivan often called on his childhood friend to assist him.

"I've had the opportunity of meeting Ms. Chandler in person, and I find her to be quite refreshing. She didn't come off as being fake to me, Onyx and I'd like to think I'm a rather good judge of character."

"Well, if you say she's okay, then I guess she's okay. She's perfect for what we need to do. In fact, the fact that Rayna went over there works well into what I have planned for Rayna. Yeah, Nyree, just made it easier to keep you a non-factor in this."

Ivan quickly spoke up, "Nah, I got plans for Nyree, so make sure she remains a non-factor in all of this." Ivan had to get a hold of Onyx. Onyx was moving in the wrong direction if he was going to try to implicate Nyree in some wrongdoing.

"IV, what are you talking about?"

"Don't worry about that Onyx. Just know that I got that under control. You've got bigger fish to fry. I am going to have fun with Miss Chandler."

"That woman has done nothing to you. I can't let you hurt her," Onyx said sternly.

Ivan laughed a sinister laugh. "What I have in mind is nothing that will be harmful. Onyx let me holler at you later. I got to get some things in motion."

"IV, I don't like the way that sounds. You didn't want her to be implicated in Operation Rayna, but yet you got plans for her. Something is not right here, and I don't like it," Onyx bluntly stated.

" The fuck you mean, you don't like it," Ivan yelled. Not waiting for a response he continued, "You ain't got to like it, Onyx. You don't get paid to like what I do or don't do. You get paid to make what I want to happen, happen. Handle Rayna, you got a little while, but don't lose sight of her. I want to know where she is day and night. If she sneezes wrong, I want to know about it. Got it."

Onyx replied dryly, "Got it," and then hung up.

NYREE CHANDLER

Nyree was agitated. Why hadn't Malachi come to see her? Why hadn't she heard from him? For all the talk she did about she didn't care what he did, or he was seeing, she did. The words were just a front to keep her from getting hurt.

"Malachi, it's me. Call me. I thought you were coming by earlier. Rayna came over here looking for you, and she was acting really bizarre. Why haven't I heard from you today? Call me and just let me know everything is okay," Nyree concluded her voice message. She felt butterflies flutter in her heart.

An anxiety attack was brewing. It had been months since she had to take any medication. A Zoloft might calm her nerves right now. Something was not right. Maybe she was anxious because she had to pull a gun on Rayna in order to get her out of her home. Her gut told her that something was not right with Malachi. Rayna had forced her way into her home demanding to see Malachi. Nyree was taken aback that Rayna had shown up at her home. She had never come to her home. Why today? Nyree wondered what made Rayna think Malachi was at her house. Rayna kept saying, "He's avoiding me, and I know you're hiding him out."

"Are you on your meds Rayna? I don't hide grown men out. What in the hell are you rambling about? Never mind get you psycho pathetic ass out my house." Nyree told Rayna. She never liked Rayna.

Nyree remembered her mother trying to mentor Rayna when they were children. As a child, Nyree complained, "Mother, stop bringing these charity cases home. Give her psychotherapy, but don't bring her here. There's no place for her in our family." Nyree still harbored bitter feelings toward Rayna. Nyree's parents were always trying to give back to the community and help those in need. Nyree was okay with that, she got it, but when it came to Rayna something just was not right with the girl. In Nyree's opinion, Rayna was the type of person who would never be satisfied. No matter how much she was given, it would never be enough.

Sad thing about it, her parents couldn't see it. Her father who always took her side had told her that she was being selfish. Nyree knew that was not the case. She could see the jealousy and envy that Rayna harbored towards her. It was funny that her mother, who gloated about being a good judge of character couldn't see it. Malachi had even been duped by Rayna. There were times when

Nyree would sit and ponder what finally made Malachi give in to Rayna. Rayna had always wanted Nyree's life. When she couldn't infuse herself into the Shaw family, it seemed that Rayna tried to have Nyree's one and only true love, Malachi. Now, that didn't seem to be working for her either.

"I'm not leaving until I see Malachi," Rayna ranted.

Nyree played along with her, "Umph humph. I hear you. Let me go see where Malachi is…" as she walked into her study and reached into the lock box in her desk, pulled out her gun and placed it in her waistband. When Nyree returned, Rayna was standing there with her hands on her hips waiting in expectation to see Malachi.

"Where is he?" Rayna demanded.

Nyree laughed," You really are psycho. Malachi isn't here. Didn't I tell you that earlier?"

"I know he's here. I saw his truck in your driveway. I know his plates. I'm not going anywhere until I talk to him."

Nyree shook her head. She and Malachi had matching vehicles same color and almost same plates. If you weren't paying close attention, you could mistake their vehicles. His personalized plate by the state of Indiana read, "CHANDLER." Nyree's personalized plates issued by the state of Indiana read, "CHNDLER."

" Oh, you will leave. Either you will walk out the door, or the coroner will carry you out. You don't want to end up like your father do you? He went into dangerous territory trying to obtain information that was not meant for him to know and now just like your daddy, you've stepped into a hostile environment looking for someone who doesn't want to be found. Like father, like daughter,

"Nyree said as she pushed her out the door. Nyree's alter ego, Ms. B was in control now. Nyree's adrenaline was pumping. The words she had spoken to Rayna were cold, cruel, and calculated. Nyree felt no regrets for having let her true feelings rise to the surface and then flow freely from her mouth. When Rayna tried to force her way back into the house, the barrel of Nyree's gun met the bridge of her nose.

"I will blow your brains clean out of your skull and allow my dogs to gnaw at your remains. Try me, Rayna."

Rayna trembled as she backed away from Nyree. After a safe distance, she turned her back on Nyree and trudged through the snow carefully. It was apparent that it was quite a feat to maneuver through the snow as another three inches of snow had fallen and the threat of being shot added to the awkwardness of her gait.

Nyree laughed as she watched the pitiful sight as she slammed her front door. *Malachi and these basic type chicks. I am too damn old for this. I've been going through this mess with him for twenty years. Enough is enough. I think I will see what Mr. Marrick has in mind. I was thinking that Malachi and I might get back together. You know what, it's time for me to move on. Vivere senza rimpianti. Live life without regrets.*

"Ivan," Nyree said as she settled onto the sofa in her living room, "you know what, I was thinking if your offer is still available I want to take you up on it."

"Well, sounds like you've had a change of heart. Yes, I was thinking I would like a good steak, and I haven't been out in a long time."

"Okay, sounds good. What time? "

"Look, Sweetheart, I want to see you and all but what happened? I mean like your boyfriend came over, y'all had an argument. What's going on? Am I going to be your diversion for the night?"

"Boyfriend? That's cute. Come on. You know I'm forty-five years old. I don't have time for games."

"Forty-five? Get the hell out of here. I thought you were like thirty-six or something like that. You're ultra fine."

"Thank you, I will be forty-five on Sunday. And how old are you because you make forty-five seem archaic?"

"Nah, I'm thirty-eight. I will be thirty-nine on my birthday… September third. I'm just saying I thought I was older than you, that's all. So back to you and your boyfriend…"

"Ivan, are you fishing for something? Do you want to know if I'm in a relationship or if I'm seeing someone?" Nyree asked.

"Damn, you don't mince no words do you?" Ivan interlocked his fingers.

"Nope. If you wanna know something, ask me. But I will tell you. I am not seeing anyone or in a relationship. My ex owns the spa, and I work with him on several projects. Once upon a time, I thought we would get back together, but we're better off being friends. The media speculates about us all the time, but he's with someone now, and they're happy. And me, I'm happy being Nyree. How about you? Who has your attention?"
"Okay, I see you. That was clever. One woman has my heart right now, and her name is Charity, but I don't know how long she is going to be around."

"Hmm. Well, why aren't you having dinner with her tonight?"

"Charity is my mother. She's in hospice. She has breast cancer, and the cancer has spread to her lungs. It's just a matter of time…" he trailed.

"Oh, no, I am so sorry. I didn't know."

"Don't ever say sorry. Say I apologize for fishing, but never sorry. When I think of sorry, I think of the following adjectives: poor, base, low, pitiful. I definitely don't think of those adjectives when I think of you. Is that how you see yourself? Don't answer because I know you don't. So, can you be ready in an hour?"

"Yep," Nyree responded.

As soon as she hung up the phone, she thought of calling back and making up an excuse about why she couldn't go. *Forget it, I'm going,* she thought as she rushed into her bedroom to rummage through her closet to see what she might wear. *If he's a jerk I never have to go out with him again,* she thought. Why now am I acting like this? In the midst of a blizzard, I decide to go on a date. This is so not me. Turning forty-five was causing her to do all manner of strange things.

IVAN MARRICK

"What?" Nyree asked Ivan as she placed her fork onto her plate. She had just eaten a mouthful of salad and found Ivan's eyes on her.

"Nothing," Ivan grinned. He sensed she didn't believe him. "Okay, here's the truth, I have not been out in a long time. You are so beautiful, and I'm just enjoying your company. I want to see you again. Is anything wrong with that? Nyree blushed. "Um," she fidgeted in her chair, folded her hands across her chest and looked down at the tablecloth, "no I guess, but we haven't finished this date yet. How do you know you are going to want to see me again?"

"You have the most beautiful smile. That little dimple you've got in your cheek, it's subtle, but it is giving me life for real. To answer your question, I've studied women. I'm like an expert of sorts on women and trust me you're one woman I am going to want to see again. I might even change your last name," He announced boldly.

"An expert on women? Is that your way of telling me you've had a lot of women in your lifetime, Mr. Marrick?"

He chuckled and let out a sigh, "Low key did you just call me a hoe?" Staring into her eyes, he looked for a response. Her eyes were not telling him anything. Continuing the conversation he told her, "Well, I've been involved with a nice amount of women in my lifetime, but I have a degree in Sociology, so I understand human behavior and under that scope, I understand women and how they think and work." Ivan's heart skipped a beat as it often did when he lied to someone unintentionally. There were certain lies he rehearsed so that they would roll off his tongue naturally. This was not one of them. What made me just tell her that I had a degree in Sociology? If she asks me where I went to school, I will say Florida A&M. Her mother is a psychologist. I sure hope she does not take the conversation into that arena. I'm a habitual liar for real. I lie sometimes just for the fun of it, but this right here is crazy.

As she smiled warmly at him, he noticed her fidget in her chair. Ivan wondered what it was that was bothering her. "Is there something wrong? Did I say something that made you uncomfortable?"

"No, you're fine. I hate to bring this up, but I'm worried about Malachi."

"Malachi…" he pretended to try to figure out who Malachi was and then snapped his finger as if the answer had magically come to him. "Your ex. I see I got competition," Ivan stated and then took a sip from his glass. The nod he gave her indicated he was up for the challenge.

Nyree waved her hands to suggest that Ivan had misunderstood her statement. "No…nah," she stuttered. Getting a grip on her speech, she continued, "Malachi and I have a relationship that is difficult to explain to outsiders. We co-parent as well as run a few businesses together. And while there is not anything romantic between us I always want the best for him. I know this may sound weird. In fact, I don't even know why I'm telling you all this. But this weather is crazy, and I haven't heard from him, and that's not like him not to call or text. We were supposed to meet today at his suggestion, and he didn't show up or call, and it was something he couldn't discuss over the phone, so I'm just a little worried."

"Oh, I see. Well, why don't you call him and see if you can get him on the phone? I'm going to go to the restroom and give you a little privacy."

"No, I will call him later," Nyree insisted.

Scooting his chair back and standing, he told her, "No, go ahead, besides I need to go to the restroom anyways. I will feel better knowing that you spoke with him and then I can have your full undivided attention. I want you all to myself. Call me a selfish bastard," he told her.

Nyree laughed politely, "No, you are so sweet, Ivan. Thank you for understanding."

"Not a problem," he said as he placed his linen napkin on the table and excused himself.

Once in the bathroom, he checked the stalls to make sure he was the only person in the restroom.

"Hey, what's up with dude?" Ivan asked as he whispered into his cell phone.

"Nothing," Onyx said, "we're still holding him at the spot. He's been in and out of consciousness."

"Where's his phone?"

"What?" Onyx asked annoyed.

"Where's the phone? Nyree is worried about him because he hasn't called or texted him. Just send her a text so she won't worry about the bastard."

"Are you serious?"

"Very much so. She's the type that would put out a missing person's report or something, so we don't need any problems. This will pacify her."

"Alright and what about Rayna?"

"Look, I gotta run, but execute that order I gave you on that situation."

Nyree smiled as Ivan returned to the table. Ivan sat down and placed his napkin back in his lap and sipped his wine. He returned the smile.

"So, I take it you spoke with him," Ivan inquired.

"No, he sent me a text saying something came up, and he wasn't able to make it. His phone has been acting up and not letting him call out, so I don't know, but I'm not going to worry about it," she told Ivan as she received a text notification. "I'm sorry, I just want to make sure this isn't a text from the kids. Excuse me as I read it."

Ivan relaxed in his chair. "No problem. Definitely want to make sure the children are fine," he stated with a bit of sarcasm, but she didn't pick up on it. Ivan quickly remembered that a woman with children was a good thing. That woman would always make sure her children were provided for as well as her man. He was glad Onyx had taken care of that matter for him. Then he noticed Nyree's face frown up as she read the text. He prayed nothing was wrong because he didn't want the night to end just yet.

"Everything okay with your angels?" Ivan inquired and even softened his tone to give the impression that he was concerned.

"It's not the kids. Malachi just sent me a text that was weird. Somebody has his phone. His response to my standard statement is absurd. I don't care where we are in the world or who we're seeing, there's only one way to respond to this statement, and he just asked me what I'm talking about."

"Maybe he didn't understand the context in which it was said," Ivan offered.

"No, we've been saying this over twenty years, the context doesn't matter. Something isn't right. Either he lost his phone, or he's in trouble. Either way, there is something wrong. I think I'm going to call the police."

"Nah, don't do that. If he lost his phone, I'm sure he will call his cell phone provider. Sometimes it takes a minute for them to disconnect the service, right?" Ivan asked nervously.

Nyree responded, "I don't know. I just know that this is not typical of Malachi."

"I will be right back, Sweetie. This wine seems to be running through me," he said as he hurried from the table.

Again checking the stalls to make sure he didn't have company, Ivan called Onyx. "What the hell dude? Don't text her again."

"I did what you asked," Onyx responded.

"Yeah, but then you did too much. She thinks it's not him. She said she made a statement to him, and you asked her what she was talking about."

"Yeah, she said something about infinity squared, and I asked what she was talking about," Onyx stated plainly.

"Okay look, don't answer the phone or text anyone else."

"Too late, I also texted the son, Carter back since you called. He didn't want anything but some money so I told him I'd get it to him."

"Carter, who the hell is Carter. They have two kids, and that boy's name is Christian. Unless they call him Carter. I don't know and not trying to find out right now. Look, you just be the goon that you are. Stop trying to play a real life person because that's not what you do and it's not working. I got to go."

"Ivan, are you okay?" Nyree asked as Ivan settled back into his seat.

"Um, yeah, why do you ask?"

"You look distracted," she said.

"Sorry, Sweetie. While I was in the restroom, I got a phone call from the facility where my mom is. She's been experiencing a lot of discomfort tonight," he told Nyree. He was relieved when the waitress started placing their meals before them on the table. He quickly changed the subject, "I see our meals have finally arrived. Let's just eat and enjoy each other's company," Ivan suggested as he watched Nyree bow her head in silence and bless her food.

Reaching down into her purse, she retrieved her Tranquil Bliss hand sanitizer and cleansed her hands. She gestured to offer Ivan some, and he held his hands out and allowed her to squirt the liquid into his hands. "What is this?" he asked as he rubbed his hands together.

She laughed, "It's hand sanitizer."

Ivan rubbed his hands together and paused before speaking. "Are you sure? I've never felt anything like this. It's so smooth and moisturizing."

"Yes. I don't know if you're familiar with Jahzara Bradley, but she's an aromatherapist and creates products for us at Chaotic Bliss. Yeah, it's not your average hand sanitizer. She doesn't make it with alcohol so it doesn't dry your skin out. I love it. This is my signature scent."

"Yeah, I know Jahz. I call her that. I got my own signature scent too. It's called Dat Dude. Jahzara that's one bad chica. She's fine…"

"Really?" Nyree raised her eyebrow, as she dropped the small container back into her bag. "Are you sure you want to stay for dinner? If you want to go check on your mom, I understand."

Ivan reached out and grabbed Nyree's hand. He drew in a breath and with exaggeration took his time to exhale. "Thank you," he whispered. Speaking only a tad bit louder he continued on, " Don't get jealous of Jahzara, she's not my type. I'd rather just eat dinner and listen to you tell me about your work, your life, your likes/dislikes or whatever... I need a distraction if you don't mind. Most of the time I'm there day and night. I love my momma. She's my heart, but I just need to replenish myself so I can be the rock she needs by her side."

"Wow, you are an amazing son."

"No. I owe her my life. I have the highest regard for women. My mother is a woman, and I know the struggle she went through to make sure I was taken care of as a child. Now I'm just trying to make sure her last days are peaceful. Don't look like that. She's going to die, and I know it, and I've made peace with it. Nyree, I'm okay with it. But I would like to talk about something else. Are you close to your mother?"

"Um...no, actually I'm not. I love my mother, but we're not close. My brother is her favorite, he can do no wrong. It's always been like that. My brother feels like I was my daddy's chosen one. You know what; my family dynamics are pretty flawed. Now my grandma, oh my, she's just a sweetheart." Nyree cut a piece of her lobster tail and chewed it, "Anyways, this lobster is to die for..."

"Maybe you and your mother can strengthen your bond. You only get one mother, and that's it. I would give anything to have things go back to the way they used to be with me and my mom. I'm so jealous of you. Your mother is able to be a part of your life and interact with you. My mother is here on this Earth, but not here, if that makes sense. Tell me about you and what you do." His eyes filled with tears. Ivan allowed a tear to drop. For the first time in his life, he allowed a woman to see his vulnerability.

"Okay, well, I happen to be able to do what I love which is buy and acquiring things. One of the projects I'm working on is to provide our youth with opportunities to come out of high school and start their own businesses."

"Really? Why that population?"

Nyree smiled, "Why not? They have a lot of energy, and I work with them in high school through my foundation and well, since Christian and India will be graduating soon, I know how important this opportunity is for our youth. With me, it's about giving back. I have been so blessed in my life, so I understand the importance of giving back. Every time I give, I'm blessed even more. What? What's that look?"

"You're not used to people looking at you?" Ivan continued to gaze at her, "Do you ever wake up in the morning and say damn, I got it going on? You shook your head no, tomorrow when you wake up do that. I was just in awe of you. I thought you were just a spoiled, privileged woman who liked to shop."

"Wow, I've been called worse and one time in life that may have been an accurate description. Children change you, though. Do you have children?"

"No, I don't. Never found a woman that I found to be worthy of being the mother of my child. With my mother being ill, I will probably not have children. I want my children to know their grandmother, and since that won't be likely, I don't desire to have children."

"What about your father?" Nyree asked.

"He's not exactly anyone I would want anyone to know. He's a functional crack head and a professional thief. He will steal the stank off shit. Very charming, but will have stolen everything from you in the blink of an eye. He and my mother are still married, but I have the power of attorney. Do you know he went to visit my mother and stole the DVD player and other electronics out of her room? I accused the facility of stealing, but when we looked at camera footage, you could see him walking down the hall with an Ipad in his hand."

"Damn," Nyree blurted out. Clearly what Ivan had said about his father was far from what she had expected to hear him say.

"I know, right. A damn shame and to think while I hate him, I carry his name." His mind drifted back to what Rayna has said about Ivan III not being his biological father. Did she know what she was talking about? It didn't matter if she did or didn't. He couldn't afford her the opportunity to spread that rumor.

"Dessert?" The waitress asked cheerily as she approached the table.

"No thank you," Nyree said as she sipped wine.

Ivan cleared his throat to get the attention of the waitress. "Yes, she is going to share some key lime pie with me," Ivan gave the waitress a wink.

"Ivan, I'm fine," Nyree waved her freshly no-chip manicured hand in protest, "but you go right ahead."

"So, you're not going to eat your favorite dessert with me?"

"How did you know?" she asked blushing again.

Ivan laughed. "I told you I study women. Plus, I read an article once where you stated it was your favorite guilty pleasure. Lisa," he said as he read the waitress' name tag, "please bring us some key lime pie with two forks and would you refresh her drink?" He placed a fifty dollar bill into her palm and told her that was for her being so attentive to them. Lisa beamed and was more than happy to oblige.

"Mr. Marrick, you're full of surprises. I am going to have dessert with you this time, but next time when I decline dessert..."

"So, there will be a next time. If you could go anywhere in the country where would it be?" Ivan was feeling good about himself.

"Orlando, I could use some warmth."

"Let's make it happen. Let's go for your birthday?" Ivan suggested.

"I don't know about that." Nyree raised her eyebrows. She was fidgeting again, and her eyelashes were fluttering.

Ivan discerned she was a little uncomfortable with the suggestion, but he continued to press the matter. "Come on, live a little. Do something different."

"That would definitely be different," she leaned forward and looked into his green eyes. Ivan sensed she was searching for something and for a moment he let his guard down and allowed her to see a human being who was vulnerable.

"Look, I don't know what you're looking for, but if you tell me what it is I can be it. I'm too old to be out in these streets playing games. I want to experience real love, build memories, and start my happily ever after right now," he told Nyree as she searched his eyes for truth.

"We shall see Ivan. I'm enjoying your company, but I'm really tired I should head home." Nyree started reaching for her designer bag.

"Nope, if you're tired don't drive. Let's go upstairs to our rooms."

"What?" Nyree questioned as they sat in T.J. Maloney's restaurant in the Radisson Hotel.

"I booked two hotel rooms here when we confirmed our plans to come here. Remember when you called earlier and tried to weasel your way out. I knew that the roads might be bad when we finished dinner, so I didn't want you to have to drive in this crap, so I took it upon myself to book some rooms. I hope you don't mind."

"Presumptuous much? But I'm too tired to argue," she told him.

Quickly, Ivan captured their waitress' attention. Once she came to the table, he informed her that he wanted to pay their bill.

"Sure, let me go print it out," she responded.

"Look here's two hundred dollars. I'm sure that should cover it as well as gratuity for you and the busboy to split," he smiled but not nearly as big as the waitress. Ivan was sure that he had left her an additional one hundred thirty dollar tip, and that was good money for the minimal amount of service she provided. But she was a kind girl, and he was reminded of the hard way he grew up.

Nyree's whole spiel about giving back to the community had warmed his heart. He and his mom had spent several nights sleeping in bus stations when his father went on drug binges. His father had caused them to lose several homes due to drugs and gambling. The memory of being trapped in an underground cave with his mother along with a dead body began to surface. He grunted.

"Ivan," Nyree gently tapped his arm, "is everything okay? You're sweating on your forehead are you okay?" Nyree asked again retrieving an unused napkin from the table and dabbing the beads of perspiration from his forehead.

He flinched as he watched her wad the napkin up and place onto the table. The gesture reminded him of his mother. "Yeah, yeah, Sweetie. I apologize for checking out on you. My mind just went back to my past when my mom was out there waitressing and trying to make it. I saw the way you looked when I told her to just keep the whole thing. No, I'm not showing out. I know what it's like to have to work hard in this world and make your way. You probably can't relate."

"You're real funny. When I graduated from college, I worked a minimum wage job and worked my way up to management. I could have went to work for my dad's company straight out of college, but I wanted to work and earn something based on my hard work not my name."

"But you are with the company today?" Ivan questioned as they walked through the lobby of the hotel.

"Hey, I said I wanted to experience some things and I did. I decided my efforts could best be put to use in the family business."

Nyree finally opened the door with the hotel key after the third time of placing the card into the slot and removing it. "Can I come in or should I just go to my room?" Ivan rocked back and forward on his heels as he waited for her response.

"Come on in and let's chat awhile. But on the first date, I never let a guy stay over."

NYREE CHANDLER

Oh, hell naw. I'm breaking all my rules. Isn't this how it started with Malachi? He stayed over on our first date because he got stranded. Now, not that I'm stranded but I'm tired, and half drunk. Okay, truth be told, I'm a lot of drunk and everybody knows I don't drive in the snow when I'm sober, so you may as well say I'm stranded. And me and Mr. Fine Marrick are going to spend the night together. I'm not going to do the nasty with him, but oh my goodness I sure can think of some things I would like to experience with him. The liquor is talking.

The words to Chris Brown's song, "Liquor" playing in her head. Had Ivan placed something in her drink when she had gone to the restroom? What did he look like underneath his clothes? She just wanted to see him strip and once she got a glance he could put his clothes back on. Nyree had no intentions of fornicating with this man, but her flesh was saying something different. Please don't let me say any of this out loud. This room is beautiful. I just want to slip out of my clothes and under the covers, but I don't have anything to slip into.

"What's wrong? You can put me out and tell me to go to my room when you get tired. I promise to be the perfect gentleman. I won't make a move on you if that's what you're thinking. Are you having second thoughts about staying the night here?" Ivan asked as he jumped onto the king sized bed. It was a move she would have expected from a child not a grown man. It made her giggle.

"Yes. I'm thinking I like your company," she slurred her words as she placed her purse onto the dresser. She allowed herself to lean on the furniture until she felt steady with her balance. Taking in the full scope of the room she continued as she slipped her Ralph Lauren leather boots off, "I definitely want to spend more time with you, but I've just never done anything like this on the first date. And I'm wishing I had some night clothes to put on. And quite honestly, I believe I've had one drink too many," she wagged her index finger repeatedly, "and tomorrow when I'm sober I may think this whole thing is a bad idea," Nyree said as she plopped onto the bed next to Ivan.

" I'm glad I could be your *first*," he teased as he emphasized the word first. His face was illuminated by his smile when he said, "Let's go to WalMart since that's the only thing open at this time and get you something to sleep in or are you too good for Dub-Mart?" Ivan questioned.

"Did you low key just call me bougie? I shop at WalMart. Are you driving?" Nyree rolled her eyes at him as she jumped up and stumbled over to the dresser to grab her Kate Spade handbag. He had insulted her with his comment. There was always someone making assumptions about her. This dude knew nothing about her.

"Look, I'm going to be honest with you. I'm probably not like the other guys you've dated. I have had a few traffic run-ins with the law, so my license is not really right, but I will drive because I don't want you to have to drive. Matter of fact, let me go pick up some items because you don't look like you feel so hot. No need for both of us to have to brave the elements. Any particular color you like? What size should I pick up? Don't give me that look. I want you to be comfortable. I don't want to pick something that would be too big or too small. I always get in trouble when I try to guess a woman's age, shoe size, and clothing size. My momma told me it was a simple way to avoid getting in trouble with this. You know what she told me?" Ivan asked.

He had her full attention. While shaking her head to indicate that she was clueless, she said, "Nope, I have no idea. What did she say? Maybe I can pass the same advice to my son."

Ivan laughed. "Yeah, you can pass the advice on to him. I wished my momma had told me this when I was your son's age. I would've avoided so many slaps and cursing-outs. So she simply told me don't guess. Ask the lady and tell her why I wanted to know."

Nyree let her eyes drift upward and to the right as if she were really thinking hard about what Ivan had just said. "Well, yeah.

That makes sense. To answer your question just get me a large and any color is fine," she told Ivan.

Ivan refocused the conversation and announced, "I will pick up a couple of toothbrushes, toiletries, and lingerie. No, I'm just kidding. You should have seen your face. I will buy you some lingerie, just not tonight, though. Okay, Sweetie, let me go ahead and make this run and I will be right back. If you want room service, feel free to order what you want. Money is never an object with me. When you're with me, you can have whatever you want. If I got it, you got it. You'll never open your purse when you're with me. I will even let you hold my Black card."

"Really?" Nyree asked.

"Really. I mean if you had to use it I'm sure it would be for a worthy cause and not just something frivolous. I got you."

"You got me," Nyree said part statement part questioning.

"Ummph, stop it. I see what you're doing. You're testing me. I will prove myself to you in due time. Give me a hug so I can go make this run, please."

Nyree gave him a hug as if he were one on the old ladies at church. Ivan was not having it. He drew her in close to him and she melted in his arms. His body awakened some parts of hers. As she eased away from him, he gently brushed her lips with his lips. She allowed her mouth to part so that his tongue could play with her tongue. Gentling pushing away from his embrace, she allowed her eyes to meet with his eyes. A spark had been ignited, and she was not so sure that she wanted it to die out.

"I'm leaving for real. Your lips are so soft," he told her as he rushed out of the door.

Nyree stood at the door for a few seconds to gain her composure. Strolling slowly over to the bed, she found herself sitting on the edge and then allowing herself to fully recline.

The tension in her shoulders melted away. Her eyelids closed, and she knew what it felt like to be in heaven. She didn't have a care in the world. Tranquil bliss is how she would have described the moment. This is what bliss felt like. Her phone rang, and her brother, Kyle's face came across the screen of her phone. It was late, and Kyle was calling, it couldn't be good. *Oh my God, please let the kids be okay. Please let my mother be okay. Please let Grandma Lula be okay and please don't let Kyle have done something stupid. Tonight, I just can't*, she found herself praying. The last time she was in a hotel room, and Kyle called she found out that her father had died.

"Hello," she answered nervously.

"Hey Sister Girl, what's up? I came by your house, and you didn't answer the door. Your truck was gone. I know the kids are at Mom's, I was just wondering if you were okay?"

Letting out a sigh, she told him, "Uh, yeah, I'm okay." She hoped he would leave it at that and not ask any more questions.

"Yeah. I mean you're out on one of the worst nights of the year?"

"Um, yeah, I went out on a date, and I'm staying at the Radisson tonight. I should be home tomorrow."

"Whoa, what? Date, who is this dude? And Malachi is cool with this?" Kyle asked. He was not the type to beat around the bush.

"Ivan Marrick. It's not Malachi's business who I see. Kyle, this time, I've moved on. He stood me up this morning and then tonight he brushed me off in a text, so I've moved on. Forget Malachi."

"So what did he say about standing you up? And Ivan Marrick, really? Isn't he too old for you? I heard he was on heroin or something like that."

"He didn't say anything. In fact, I've called him a couple of times, and he never picked up, but he finally texts me and said he's been busy, and he'll get up with me when he can. And Ivan Marrick the fourth, not the third. You're real funny with that."

Kyle chuckled," Okay, I was like whoa, she done went out and got a Sugar Daddy. Haha. Oh, all I knew was the one who Dad used to work with years ago. I heard he had a gambling problem. Lost not one, but several homes in foreclosure. So, I'm guessing there's a son and how did it come to be you, and the son would end up on a date and in a hotel? How long have you been seeing this guy? I talk to you almost every day, and you've never mentioned him."

"Nosey much? Dang, We've had coffee a couple of times and lunch a few times. Nothing came of it. Then today he was at the spa and asked me out, and I was like okay. It's kind of our first date, but not really if that makes sense. I gotta get off the phone before he gets back. He went to WalMart, and if it makes you feel better, we got separate rooms."

"Really, so how did the receptionist look when she saw him and you standing there and paying for two hotel rooms?"

"He got the rooms before I arrived here. He said he thought it might be too bad to drive, and he booked them in advance."

"This dude running game on you. He booked two rooms in advance. Get the hell out of here," Kyle laughed and continued, that sounds like one of my lines from back in the day. Nyree, It's only one room. He is really smooth. How much do you know about this dude? I don't think it's good to spend the night in the room with him. And he's gone to the store, for what? I don't like the sound of this, Nyree."

"Kyle, I had a buzz, and now you're blowing it. I wasn't planning on staying the night, and he went to pick up a night shirt and some other stuff."

"Okay, look, here's what you do. You put your keys, credit card, and license in your bra and you sleep in your bra. When he gets back, you can chat with him and then make him go to his room. You know you sleep like a log. This is a perfect set up for a robbery. I'm guessing you would feel someone going in your bra that's why you keep those items close to you. Call me if you need me. I don't like this one bit. Why are you so trusting of people, Nyree? You're always giving somebody the benefit of the doubt. That's how you always end up in these relationships with these crazed and deranged people. Remember Colin Jordan? Malachi to be truthful don't always play with a full deck either, but he's mellowed out a lot. Twenty years ago I was going to pop him off something real nasty. The only thing that saves him now is like I said he has mellowed out and he's the father of your kids."

Nyree hadn't heard anything else Kyle said after he mentioned Colin Jordan. His name caused her anxiety. She had been to see him a couple of times while he was in prison. He seemed remorseful for what he had done. They had talked about business during those visits. He still had the knack for business and had given her some good advice. Next month she was due to speak at Colin's parole hearing. Her heart was beating fast. The thought of Colin being set free and now her brother had her thinking that Ivan might be some deranged lunatic. She had read about people meeting up with people from the internet and getting robbed, but this was crazy. Could Kyle be right? What if Ivan was buying zip ties, duct tape, and stuff to kill her? He had been gone for quite some time. WalMart was just down the road he probably should be back by now.

"Yeah, I will talk to you later," Nyree said as she pressed the end button on her screen. With haste she made her way into the bathroom, she washed her hands and began shoving every item she could possibly get to fit into her bra cups. Carefully she adjusted the items in her bra so that they would not cause any unnecessary bulging. Her brother had her paranoid. Was she really naïve? She removed the items from her bra, put them back in her purse and set the purse on the nightstand. She refused to go through this with Ivan. For a brief time while when she was married to Malachi, she had to hide money in sanitary napkin boxes, underneath meat in the freezer, and other places. Nyree told herself that she would just have to sleep lightly in case Ivan decided to tiptoe back in her room later tonight, but she didn't anticipate a problem.

"Hey Sweetie, it is cold as hell out there. People were buying up WalMart. That's the next thing I'm going to buy...a Dub Mart. I thought owning a gas station was the lit, but nah, Dub Mart got it going on. It is snowing even harder than it was earlier. They're telling people not to travel and be on the roads if they don't have to be. Part of I-65 has been shut down. We may just have to stay here tomorrow too. I'm not lying. You should be getting the weather alerts on your phone. I bought you some jogging pants, underwear, and I thought this bra would be cute for you," he trailed as he began taking the contents out of the bags and putting them on display.

"Wow, thank you, Ivan. You are so thoughtful. I never thought about what I would do in the morning for clean clothes," she lied. She kept what she called a "get-a-way" bag in her trunk. It had an extra set of clothing in it, a blanket, water, soap, deodorant and toothbrush along with toothpaste. The only thing it didn't have was pajamas which she had noted she would add. There was also a bag in the trunk for India and Christian.

"You're welcome. I hope you liked my choices, that's partly what took me so long. I have not had the opportunity to shop for a woman in a long time. I mean I pick up items for my mom, but a woman that I'm interested in romantically, yeah, it's been awhile."

"So, you're interested in me romantically?" Nyree questioned as she folded the items and placed them in the drawers.

"Nope," he teased, "I like you like a sister."

"Really, let me see," she teased as she inched over to where he was sitting on the bed and allowed her lips to brush his. He pushed her down on her back and got on top of her and kissed her deeply.

He pulled away and whispered, "I want you. I'm not going to lie, but what I want more than anything is a friendship---a relationship. You're different from the women I usually encounter. At dinner, I enjoyed our conversation about the state of America and the Black community. You challenged my ideas and thoughts, and I think I challenged yours as well. I'm not here for sex. I want it all."

Nyree was flustered as she turned from his gaze. He was still on top of her and adjusted her face so that they were looking eye to eye. "You've never met anyone like me, have you? I'm not afraid to tell you what I want and how I want it. Don't run from this. You want to know if I'm full of shit or if I'm the real thing. Try me and find out," he told her as he got up and walked to the drawer where she placed her pajama top and bottom set he had just purchased. Ivan placed the items on the bed.

"Go take a shower, put on your pajamas and call me when you finish. If you need me, don't hesitate to let me know. I'm here for you tonight and any other night that you might need me," he declared as he walked to the door.

"Okay," was all she could manage to utter as he opened the door and went to his room. Nyree quickly gathered the toiletries, her handbag, and the pajamas and went into the bathroom and locked the door. *I think I'm in love,* she thought to herself.

After she had showered, she sat wrapped in the plush terry cloth towel on the bed. She was glad that she had her purse-sized "Sweet Thang" Body Smoothie and the matching body spray by Jahzara Bradley. Her skin craved moisture all year round but in the winter even the more. Jahzara Bradley's Tranquil Bliss line made her feel luxurious.

"Hey Ivan," Nyree whispered into the phone receiver in her hotel room, "guess what I'm doing?"

"Hmm. I don't know, Sweetie. What are you doing? Are you thinking about me?"

"Yep," Nyree said and then became distracted by the notification of an incoming text on her cell phone. Checking it, she saw it was a text from Malachi that said, "What's up?" She flicked her wrist and tossed the phone on the bed. *Really? What's up? I'm done,* Nyree told herself as she refocused on Ivan. "So, I just wanted to call and thank you for tonight and everything. I don't think I told you thank you."

"You're welcome, Sweetie. I just want you to be comfortable when you're with me."

Nyree played with the ends of her hair. Her hairstylist had cut a little more than she was comfortable with, but it was a becoming haircut nonetheless. "So, what are you doing?"

"Actually, I was just playing around with a beat and getting ready to buy these tickets to Orlando for us."

"What?" Nyree questioned.

"I'm taking you to Orlando this weekend for your birthday," he told her.

"No, no, Ivan, I can't go to Orlando with you," she told him plainly.

Not accepting, "no" for an answer he asked her, "Why not? It'll be fun."

Rolling her eyes at the ceiling, she responded, "I like you. Don't get me wrong, but we barely know each other. It's too soon."

"You're staying in a hotel with me tonight. So what's the difference between us staying in Merrillville, Indiana or Orlando, Florida?" He asked as if he had presented a valid and logical argument.

Her head was beginning to pound. The circumstances would be totally different. In fact, this was a happenstance. It just so happened that they were dealing with inclimate weather that caused this occurrence. Under normal conditions, this would not be happening. He was very persuasive, and she could tell he was not used to being told, "no," but she was going to draw her line in the snow here. This had gone too far. A little outing to get out of the house, do something different and get her mind off of Malachi was becoming stressful quickly. Nyree decided to take a different approach with Ivan.

"You know it's not like that," she whined.

"You're concerned about what people will say and think. Screw what they think. Here's what I am suggesting a birthday weekend in sunny Orlando at a resort, Mystic Dunes. Two bedrooms so you will have your own room and if you want to come over to my room..."

"Ivan, that sounds good but..."

"But nothing. I just booked the tickets and the resort while we were talking, so you can't back out."

Nyree heard tapping at her door and bolted up. She looked out the peephole and saw Ivan holding his laptop. She beamed as she opened the door.

"Hey Sweetie," he returned the smile as he closed his burner phone. It's 2016, and he's using an antiquated phone. Nyree found that curious. He's on a Mac Book, but talking on an outdated phone. It didn't add up. She was not materialistic or thought that a phone brand spoke to a person's character, but just looking at how flamboyant Ivan was it definitely raised her eyebrow.

"So, let me show you the flight times and email you our itinerary," he said as he made himself comfortable on the king-sized bed.

Nyree watched his feet in his Nike flip flops sway back and forth. Where had the shoes come from? WalMart don't sell those. What was the probability that he was driving around with summer footwear in his car? He was becoming questionable real quick. Nyree followed him to the bed and just listened. *Oh God, what have I gotten myself into?*

"Thank you, Ivan. I'm sure we will have fun," she told him.

"Do you get to Florida often?" he asked.

"Umm, actually I do. You know my ex, and I used to live in Florida, and my mom is from Florida, so it's like a second home. I am a silent owner in a venture in Jacksonville, so I'm actually down there quite a bit checking on my investment." She wanted to tell him about her grandfather whom her mother had stashed away in a nursing home for years and lied about his existence. After all, he had shared with her about his mother and father, but something in her told her to keep quiet about it.

"Impressive. And I thought you were only into ventures here in the Midwest."

"Well, what about you, Mr. Marrick, what do you do?"

"I am revamping my dad's construction business, and I'm in the music industry. I own a record company, Musically Inclined. We manage a couple of groups out of Atlanta. I own a few pieces of real estate in Atlanta and some property here in the Midwest. I'm in the process of acquiring some beachfront property."

"Sweet. Yes, I love the lake front property. I have a few pieces that have allowed me to be able to sit pretty. Casino owners and other investors are constantly after me about selling but, no, I like the idea of having something valuable someone else wants."

"You definitely have some goods that I want," he said suggestively.

"Is that right, Ivan?"

"Yeah, that's right. Ivan just seems so impersonal. Call me IV. It's what people close to me call me."

"Okay, IV," Nyree tested the name out. Positioning her body to face him she asked, "So tell me what you are interested in?"

Ivan smiled at her and inched in close to her. He told her, "I'm not who you think I am. I am not even sure I can be who you want me to be. I know women. I've studied women. I have taken lots of sociology classes at the University. Right now you're trying to see how far I will go. I'm a man. I' m going to test your limits. I am going to go as far as you let me and convince you to let me go past that point," he stroked her cheek, then moved down to her breast and right to the center of her womanhood. She gave him a look that suggested she was surprised he had gone to that place.

"That's what you wanted to know, but not quite bold enough to ask," Ivan told her, "you got freaky tendencies, but don't want anyone to know. It's cool with me. You can be a lady in public and

98

freak in the sheets. You fuck with me you're going to need your hair done after every session. Yeah, I'm that sure of myself. I'm that dude. I'm going to go back to my room," he told her and then passionately kissed her and got up to go to his room.

"Not so quickly. You said you were working on a beat, I want to hear it."

"Yeah, it's just something I'm playing with, so don't laugh."

"Why would I laugh?" she questioned as she watched him open the program and he began playing it.

Bobbing her head to the beat, she took his laptop from him and began adding some instrumentals to it.

"Okay, Sweetie, I see you. What you know about this?" He gleamed.

"I know a little something, something," she licked her lips.

"My love is what you need. And Imma give you fifty shades of it," he sang over the beat. "I'mma write a song for you and since you like that movie Fifty Shades of Grey. Imma call this Fifty Shades of Gold. I'm the golden boy. I'm all you need there won't be another after me," Ivan said firmly.

"Alright, I want that Fifty Shades of Gold. When are you going to be done with it?"

"Umm, I just started playing with it. I dunno. You can't put that kind of pressure on a guy."

"Why not? You were just talking about how you can deliver, and you're the golden boy, right. You're the golden boy, deliver." Nyree said with feistiness.

"I'm about to go back to my room," he teased.

"I'm not ready for you to leave. Let's see if we can find something on Netflix because there isn't anything of interest on television."

"Cool. Netflix and Chill or we could make our own Fifty Shades movie? Don't look at me like that," he laughed as he smacked her voluptuous behind.

MALACHI CHANDLER

"Can, I get you something?" The nurse asked Malachi as he lay in bed.

He winced as he exhaled. His head pounded so hard that he thought his brain was going to jump out his head. He had endured several hits to his ribs by a Louisville slugger and every breath he drew reminded him of the ordeal. To say he had gotten his ass whipped would be an understatement. Was it a random act or violence or was it orchestrated by someone who had a personal vendetta against him? Who and why were questions he didn't have answers for at this moment? Was this because of his fame and status as a rapper or was this related to some of his past actions?

"Get rest," is all he kept hearing the nurses and his children tell him. How could he rest? His life was in danger. Even though the Hobart Police Department was working to find the culprits and a guard was posted at the door to his hospital room, fear pumped through his body. Nyree was not returning calls, and he began to wonder if she might be behind this. Paranoia was another illness he was suffering from. Or was it that heifer, Rayna who did this to me? Her words kept replaying in his head, "Malachi, you're definitely going to pay, in more ways than one."

"Yes, can I get something for pain?" He finally answered the nurse with a question. The last seventy-two hours of his life were a blur. He had been beaten by his captors, tied up and left for dead slumped over the steering wheel of his truck. Eternally grateful is what he would be for the person who found him and called the Hobart Police when they spotted his truck in the parking lot of the fitness center. His angel told detectives he wished to remain anonymous. Malachi couldn't blame the individual for not wanting to come forward, after all, that person had witnessed first hand the aftermath of what could happen if you crossed the captors.

Lying in his hospital bed, hooked up to oxygen and IV machines was almost déjà vu for him. He recalled the last time he had been confined to the hospital. That had been when his former brother-in-law, Kyle Shaw, stabbed him in the abdomen. This attack was different though it seemed more malicious.

His captors had given him ketamine, a drug used in animals like anesthesia. According to one of the nurses on staff he had been K-holing. He had been having out of body experience while being fully awake. He should have been in a lot of pain when they left him in the truck in sub zero weather, but the drugs were so powerful and infused into his system that he didn't feel the effects of the hypothermia. However, now his body was fully awakened to every touch and sensation. His skin looked horrific.

Malachi couldn't rest because he was trying to piece together the event of the ordeal. After Rayna left his house, he had gone back to his bedroom to rest. Then there was the call from the school informing him of the early dismissal. Apparently, the school hadn't been able to reach Nyree. Where had Nyree been that she couldn't answer her phone? Nyree would drop anything for her children. That was totally out of character for Nyree, he recalled having thought at the moment. He had cursed that every time he dozed off his sleep was being interrupted. Even though it had been around nine-thirty, he just wanted a few more minutes to sleep. That didn't happen because of some pounding on the door. He remembered rushing to the door without checking the camera, thinking it was Rayna on the other side of the door.

"You got to stop coming over here. We're over," he shouted while opening the door. He was taken aback to find two young men with shovels standing before him. His mind was racing, and he only heard a portion of what one of them said regarding shoveling his driveway.

"Nah, I'm good," he told them as he attempted to close the door. It seemed odd that they didn't turn in the opposite direction. One guy pushed the door back, and the other one had his coat wide open showing Malachi a pistol.

"Well, come on in," Malachi told them in a sarcastic tone.

One of the men told Malachi to unarm the security system and not to do anything stupid. Malachi was certain the cameras had picked the men up when they were outside, so he did as instructed. They spoke well, and he was certain that these were sophisticated goons who had been sent to take him out.

"I'm not dying today. Nope. I got too much to live for. In a few hours, I am going over to Nyree's house and let her know how life is going to unfold. We're too old to be doing this back and forth dance that we've been doing for years." He told himself and rehearsed part of what he would tell Nyree when he saw her. Malachi was going to make her Mrs. Chandler all over again, and she accepted. Malachi was that confident of himself. Plus, the three karat chocolate diamond ring would win her over. That was for certain.

"What is this all about?" Malachi remembered asking, "Money? You want money? I can get you money. Let me go to my safe."

Their faces were covered by the hooded hats they wore. The one with the raspy voice laughed and said, "Nah, this isn't about money. This is about principles. See you've upset the equilibrium of things. You go around doing what you feel you're big and bad enough to do. You satisfy urges, but never think about how your taking affects the whole scheme of things."

"Man, that's profound, but I'm sure you didn't come to my house to drop knowledge on me, my brother," Malachi responded sarcastically.

The other one who was less talkative said, "Sit you ass down and shut the fuck up," as he smacked Malachi across the face. Satisfied that he had Malachi's attention, the man of few words cleared his throat and continued, "Here's what's going to happen.

We're going to set some things right today. See you've taken more in life than you've given. The universe has been kind to you, even though you've met Karma a few times you really shouldn't be here. You destroyed a prominent businessman in this city. You sold him drugs. That was wrong. Some people should be off limits. You've run through more women and mistreated them…"

"Wait so you break in my house because I used to be a drug dealer and you think I've had too much pussy in my life. I am not going to be punished for supporting my financial and sexual appetites."

Raspy voice pulled his gun out while the other goon punched Malachi several times in the face and in the nose. Raspy voice fired a shot near Malachi's foot, but it missed. "Now, as I said before sit your ass down. I think we've made our point. Now, we're going to torture you slowly before we kill you. I'm going to do you just like we used to do those bastards we had to deal with when we were in Desert Storm. You've been given too many chances in life to get it right. Your appetite, as you so eloquently put it has put you in a bad position."

Malachi tried to remember more, but the last image he re-membered was being tied up at gunpoint. He tried to use positive mental talk, but his body went into fright mode, and urine began to trickle down his leg. One of the most vivid images from the ordeal was having a foreign substance injected into his veins. The less talkative one obviously had some medical training. He put on the gloves and removed them as he had seen nurses here in the hospital dispose of them. The way he tied the tourniquet, used his index finger to trace his veins to make sure it was a good spot, tapped the needle and inserted the substance was all done in a professional manner.

****

"Dad, Dad!" he heard India calling him as he allowed himself to drift back into the present moment.

He heard her, but it was taking him longer to process what people were saying to him. Staring at her intently, he answered slowly, "Yes, Honey. Why are you yelling?"

Playing with her ponytail nervously, she wrinkled her nose, voice wavering she responded, "Dad, I've been standing here for nearly ten minutes, and you've been staring at me. I've called out to you several times, and it's like you didn't hear me. I don't know how you couldn't hear me, though. Then you just started shaking uncontrollably."

The nurse rushed in and began taking vitals. "Malachi, how do you feel?" she asked.

He gave her a puzzled look. "Have you been my nurse all day?" He didn't recognize her, and she spoke as if she were familiar with him. Malachi was shaking.

"Yes, I've been with you since six this morning. I will be leaving when my shift is over at three, so I have about two more hours with you. You don't remember me coming in and checking on you and us walking around the room and talking about your goals?" She asked almost with a tinge of disappointment.

Rubbing his eyes briskly, he blinked. His vision was blurry, "I'm sorry. There is so much going on in my mind. I can't discern what's real and what's not. Do you know where my contacts are?

India, where in the hell is your mother, did you ever get her on the phone?"

"How are you feeling?" the nurse asked once again.

"I'm good," he answered annoyed. He was alive but not sure what his quality of life was going to be. The pain he felt couldn't be described. The mental anguish he was experiencing was beyond belief. He felt abandoned. It was not just because he had been left for dead in subzero weather. His mother hadn't come to see him, she claimed the weather was too bad. Nyree was unavailable and every time he asked India about it, she seemed to never respond. He was making a mental note to himself to not let her avoid answering his question.

"So, yeah what did you mother say?"

"Well, I called her, and she said…"

"Whoa, whoa, wait, is that Rayna's picture. What's going on?" he asked.

Malachi's attention then focused on the television with the "BREAKING NEWS ALERT" on the bottom of the screen and a picture of Rayna. "Rayna Summers has gone missing. She has not shown up to her local Gary, Indiana television station since Tuesday. Staff members state it is not like her to not show up or call. Police state they are in the midst of an investigation, but would not comment further."

"I'm not a conspiracy theorist, but this just seems pretty coincidental don't you think? I get kidnapped, held hostage, whatever the hell you want to call it in my house. Then during the same time frame, Rayna goes missing. It's one of two things. She was behind what happened to me and trying to cover her tracks or the same people who did what they did to me have done something to her. Either way, she's connected to this some kind of way. Are the police still out there guarding my room?"

India stared at Malachi in confusion as he vented. Letting out a sigh, India mumbled, "Yeah. Mom will be back Monday."

"Wh.. What's today?"

"It's Saturday. Tomorrow is her birthday."

"T...T...Tell me again, wh...where is she? Who is she with?"

"You know what, I'm sick of...my whole life you all have put us in your bullshit. One minute you all love each other and the next you all are seeing other people and want me and Christian to report back to you what the other person is doing. We don't want to be put in that position. We don't want to see one parent hurt by the other parent, but this shit just got old today. She went to Disney World with her new boyfriend whom we met once at the spa. So there you have it. I'm going home, I have an exam Monday. Feel better," she told her father and stormed out the door and slammed it.

He stared at the door and cried. Hearing it, slam caused him to feel rejected as he had felt so many times in his life. Growing up without a father around and a mother not emotionally available to him, caused him to feel rejected. Nyree had always been so attentive to him. He was not used to a woman being attentive to him. Instead of appreciating it, he constantly found himself hurting her before he could be hurt by her. In recent years his mother and brother hadn't been around much unless it benefited them financially. When he wrote his tell-all book "Confessions of a Player" that put him on the best seller's list and money in his pocket, his mother and brother then started coming around more. Malachi winced in pain as he thought about the last time he saw his mother. She had come over to his home. "Son, all I need is a start-up investment for this business, and I know it will be successful."

"Yeah," he had responded.

"Yes, I will pay you back."

"No, need. I am going to write you this check and then lose my number. Don't call me anymore. I only hear from you when you want something," he scribbled on the check, and that was the last he had seen of her. Even now he didn't want to see her.

Tears flowed down his face as his head throbbed. He recalled listening to India's conversation with Nyree.

"So, after all I said happened to Dad, you're not coming home? You can't get a flight out. Oh, you will be back on Monday. But you could celebrate your birthday here. Okay, see you Monday."

Refusing to deal with the emotional and physical pain any longer, Malachi pressed the red call button attached to his bed. He heard the nurse over the intercom call, "Yes!"

"I need something for pain. I know I should be able to get something now," he snapped.

"Let me check your chart and see when the last time you had something. If you can have something, I will bring it down. Do you need anything else?"

"No, just the pain medication," he snapped again. His anger was not at the nurse, but since she was the only person he could lash out at she got it.

NYREE CHANDLER

The announcement came over the intercom to return the trays to the upright position. "Southwest would like to thank you for traveling with us on today. We will be landing at Chicago Midway Airport in about twenty minutes. Please remain seated with your seatbelt on," Nyree heard the man's voice saying as she slowly awakened. Ivan began gently shaking her. "Sweetie, we're almost home," he was telling her as she fidgeted in her seat and made eye contact with him. Her ears felt stuffy.

She yawned, hoping to clear her head, "Um, yeah, okay," she told him without much emotion.

"Are you okay? You slept most of the flight, and you were very quiet this morning at breakfast."

"Perfect," she responded dryly as she rolled her eyes. *What the hell does he want me to say? He made us late getting to the airport this morning, and we nearly missed our flight. I got detained by TSA because I didn't look like my Indiana driver's license. I lost forty pounds, and I guess that did make me look like a different person. And I guess it didn't help that I dyed my hair jet black and ditched the curly sew-in hairstyle didn't help. So, yeah, I'm a little irritated.*

"We made the flight, damn, live a little. Everything doesn't have to be scripted in life. If we missed the plane, we just would've caught another flight. That damn simple."

"Did I say anything about you prancing in the mirror more than me and that's what made us late? I said I'm good."

"Here you go with those gay innuendos. I told you I'm straight. Just because my nails are healthy and longer than yours don't mean shit. I know a lot about fashion and like my shoes to match my shirts and they have to be the same name brand, but that means nothing. Maybe I'm anal, but I'm not gay."

"Umph huh," was all Nyree nodded slowly, while squinting her eyes at him.

"Really, Nyree, that's what you let come out your mouth. You didn't think I was gay when I wined and dined you. You didn't think I was gay when I bought you that Breitling watch for your birthday and took you on this expensive vacation," he ranted.

Taking off the watch, holding it in her hand, she responded, " You know what, you insisted that we take this trip. That's my fault. I should have went with my first mind and not gone on this trip with you but no, I let you convince me. I go to Florida all the time, so getting on a plane and going to Florida is nothing for me.

You bought me a birthday present. I buy myself nice stuff all the time and my friends buy me nice gifts, and I buy them nice gifts as well. So, what you did is what I'm used to. Apparently, it's an exception to your rule. Maybe you have buyer's remorse," she paused as she began to twirl the timepiece in her hand. "Take this watch," she told him as she opened his hand and placed it into his hand. Her voice became louder, "I got money and don't need yours. I can't be bought. You're the **one** bringing up things about your behavior that makes it suspect. If you were gay or not, I wouldn't care. However, I thought a heterosexual man was trying to embark in a relationship with me. I don't do drama or compli-cated. And since you're on a roll let's talk about you twerking in the Parliament House last night all up on that dude. That's what made me question your sexuality."

Nyree noticed that it seemed to be a myriad of cell phones pointed in their direction. Ivan fumed as he began to realize what had just taken place. His eyes flashed hatred toward Nyree.

"Nope," she told him as she reached under the seat to make sure her purse was in place. As she reclined in the seat, "Not my fault and you won't make me feel guilty for this. You should have left good enough alone when I said I was perfect. You embarked upon this conversation."

"I don't want to argue with you and definitely not here. You know you've been acting funny ever since you found out your ex was hurt and in the hospital."

"Leave Malachi out of this. He has nothing to do with this. Matter of fact, never mind… we can table it for another time if you'd like, Mr. Marrick," she said as politely as she could. He had really just irritated her. Malachi, from what she understood from her children and the online newspaper was left at death's doorstep, and Ivan had the audacity to bring it up because she was not being ingratiating toward him.

"Nyree, you've been giving me attitude all day. It's cool. Give me your arm," he said taking it and putting the watch back on it. "If I buy you something you can't give it back. I don't care how pissed you are."

It was a bumpy landing. She found herself praying for a smooth landing without incident. The pilot came over the intercom. "Alright, folks we have landed at Chicago Midway. Once again we thank you for flying Southwest Airlines. If you're vacationing in the Windy City, we say welcome, and if you're returning home, we say 'Welcome Home.' Local time is 12:41 pm. It's partly cloudy with a temperature of forty-five degrees."

As soon as they were allowed to release their seatbelts, she eased down the aisle and made her way off the plane. She yelled back to Ivan, I will catch up with you at baggage claim, I got to make it to the restroom. Nyree hurried into the restroom and fixed her make-up. At baggage claim, she was able to obtain her luggage quickly. When she stood up after inspecting the name tag on the bag she retrieved, Ivan was standing right there in her face. He lifted her chin up and kissed her on the lips. Nyree rolled her eyes. He kissed her again. She rolled her eyes again. He kissed her again, this time allowing his tongue to slip into her mouth. This time, she slightly cut her eyes at him. He whispered, "You know I am just going to keep doing this until you smile."

Nyree sighed. Ivan kissed her again and drew her body into his. "Okay," she protested. He was displaying an inordinate amount of public affection.

"You still mad at me?" he asked.

"Who said I was mad at you?"

"You were. I just survived my first argument with you. You hungry? You haven't eaten since lunch yesterday."

"I'm tired, and I don't travel well under stress," she lied as they walked to another area of baggage claim to retrieve their golf clubs. When she finally saw their bags, she was relieved. Her father had bought her those Taylor Made clubs and the bag and she cherished them.

Her stomach began turning flips. She prayed she would not vomit. Nyree was sick to her very core. Ivan was holding her jacket and suggested that she put it on. It was forty-five degrees outside, but now she was perspiring. *I know I'm not about to have a hot flash. She had never had one before, but the way she was feeling is what she imagined a hot flash would be like.* Why was it that every time she went out of town with a guy some tragedy happened?

Her mind drifted back to sixteen years ago when she and Malachi had gone to New York to shoot a video for one of his songs. Her father died while she was in New York. She recalled how she and Malachi had taken a red eye flight. It was just like yesterday the way the scene played out in her head. She recalled standing in the very area that she's currently standing in now. It seemed as though, no sooner than she had retrieved her bags, did the cameras start flashing. Every local newspaper reporter and news station seemed to be there trying to get a comment. She hoped that

115

no one would be there to ask about Malachi. She calmed her nerves with the thought that it would not be that easy for outsiders to be in the airport now. Security had heightened and changed. Nyree knew that people would do anything to cover a breaking story, but then she had to remind herself that this really was not about her so she would be fine. Sometimes she had delusions of grandeur.

"Sweetie, are you okay? You don't look well. Wait right here by the door for me and I will go out here and see if our limo driver has arrived. I texted him and told him that our flight was on time and to be here at 1:30. I accounted for the baggage pick up."

"Thanks, Ivan. I will be right here on this bench. I apologize I just don't feel well," she fanned herself rapidly.

"No problem. I will just take the bags with me and dash back in. Do you want me to take your carry-on bag with me?"

"Yes," she started and then said, "no, I think I may have some mints at the bottom I can dig out to settle my stomach."

She pretended to rumble through the bag looking for them as she watched him make his way to the door. Right before they left the resort he had been zipping her carry-on bag up. She had found it strange at the time, but because they were in such a hurry, she didn't pursue it. Nyree was sure he had put something in her bag, and now he wanted it back, but what was it? When she continued to scurry through the bag, there was a white envelope neatly tucked at the bottom. She opened it and lost count after counting thirty-one hundred dollar bills. Who in the hell travels with that much cash? Another thing that piqued her curiosity was that Ivan always paid for everything in cash.

Nyree didn't travel with her major credit cards, but she did transfer money to a card issued by the bank for the purpose of traveling. It allowed her to transfer money from her checking accounts to the card. It gave her a sense of security knowing that if it were lost or stolen it was not her life's fortune that had been stolen. Using the card allowed her to track her expenses without worrying about receipts. Ivan, on the other hand, didn't seem to want to track online.

He doesn't have a digital footprint. No social media. An email that is not easy to associate with him. He doesn't even use the internet on his phone. He constantly wants to use my phone to search things on the internet. He's hiding something or avoiding something, but what?

"Did you find the mints?" He touched her shoulder.

Nyree flinched. "No, apparently I ate them all. Is the driver here?"

"Yes. I put a package in your bag, and I will need to get that out when we get in the limo."

"I saw that. What is that all about?" She asked as they settled into the limo.

"Some things you should not question."

Nyree slid away from Ivan and allowed her head to recline on the seat and stretched her legs out. She closed her eyes and prayed that the driver got her home safe and sound. Even with her eyes shut, she could sense Ivan had closed the gap that she purposely put between them. When his hand grabbed her thigh aggressively she opened her eyes.

"Ouch. What is wrong with you?"

"That didn't hurt," he told her.

"It did. Don't ever touch me like that," she warned.

"Or what?" he asked looking at her as if he had been possessed by a demon.

"Ivan, I'm not playing with you. Don't touch me like that ever in your life."

"Or what, Nyree, what?"

"Some things shouldn't be questioned," she whispered. Opening up the partition, she spoke to the driver, "How's traffic looking. Do you think you can take the Indiana toll road? I need to get home as soon as possible." Rolling her eyes at Ivan, she moved to the seat across from them and stretched out.

Her phone rang, "Hello this is Nyree Chandler." She listened intently to what was being said and nodded her head. Finally, she was able to get a word in, "Okay, thank you for calling. I will be in my office on tomorrow and handle the matter. Thank you for calling me."

"Are you freaking kidding me?" Nyree asked as a new call came into her phone. "Nyree Chandler. Yes, it is. Yes. And it's absolutely necessary. Well, what did he say about it? Well, I think you should at least discuss it with him. I will be there at four and then we can discuss it face to face," Nyree huffed as she hit end on the screen without saying goodbye. She had just come off vacation, but her stress level was off the charts.

"Everything okay, Sweetie?" Ivan inquired.

"No, but I will handle it. Malachi is going to need a lot of services when he gets home, and I may just bring him home with me. I need to meet with the social worker at the hospital today."

"So, y'all getting back to together? What's going on with us?"

"Ivan, did you hear me say that I am going to get back with him? Did you not see on the news that the man was left for dead in subzero weather in a truck? So, um no there is no getting back together. He has no family ties. He has not talked to his mother in years. I am the closest thing he has to family, and he constantly treats me like… you know what it's the Pisces in me that causes me to be ever forgiving and lend help to those who despitefully misuse me. I would want someone to help me in my time of need. He can't be left alone. "

Nyree sighed as she watched Ivan text on his phone. He was quiet for once and seemed preoccupied with whoever he was texting.

"Home sweet home," Nyree announced as the driver pulled into her driveway. The snow had partially melted, and she could see patches of green grass popping up. It was the second day of spring, so it needed to look like it. She wrinkled her nose as she stood at the trunk watching the driver remove her items. Ivan stood at her side with his hands in his pockets. He rocked back and forth on his heels. Wearing only a white tee and jeans, Nyree suspected that he had to be cold. This was not Florida she wanted to holler but decided against it.

"Thanks, I got it," Ivan told the driver as he retrieved Nyree's belongings and walked her to the front door of her house. Nyree pressed the alarm key fob on her key chain, unlocked the door and entered with Ivan at her heels.

"Something seems off, "she announced as she beckoned for Ivan to roll her things into the living room. As they got deeper into the living room, she noticed that paper was all over the place. It appeared that someone had ransacked her living room.

"I know my kids didn't do this," she said, disappointed. "Where is my flat screen television?" she asked as she looked on the wall where it had once hung. "Ugh, Ivan I can't believe this shit." She walked around the house and everything else seemed to be in place until she got to the family room where another television was missing along with the game systems. However, the computer, printer and everything else was in place. Running frantically through the house she checked the other rooms, and everything was fine. In her office, the safe was in place, and her personal papers were in place, along with her antique coins.

"Sweetie, are you okay? You want me to call the police?"

"No, I will do that. I don't want to hold you up," she told him as she walked him to the front door.

"How could someone break into your house and your system was on?" he asked.

Irritated about the situation and because she hadn't heeded Malachi's warning, she let out a sigh. In her head, she could hear Malachi's voice telling her, "Babe, you need more alarm sensors throughout the house, and you need some cameras. The system should be connected to your phone so you can make sure it's armed at all times. You know you're prone to forget things."

Nodding her head as if she were in agreement with what Malachi once said, she allowed herself to refocus on Ivan. Nyree told him, "I can't figure it out. No forced entry. I will get to the bottom of this. I have never had this problem. This is a quiet neighborhood. But let me let you go. I'm going to get the police over here and get some rest."

"I can stay here with you until the police come," Ivan offered.

"No, no, you need to go home and handle your affairs. Maybe I will come stay with you," she half-heartedly stated.

"Um, I would like that, but I forgot to tell you that my uncle is staying with me for a while. He's legally blind, and my home is very modest. In fact, I'd be ashamed for you to come there," he told her.

"Ivan, stop lying. If you live with a female, just say that. This blind uncle and my house is a mess is a cover up for something. You know what, this weekend was fun. Apparently, it's over, and that's cool, but don't lie to me. Ain't nobody got time for that mess." Nyree pushed him out the door.

"I'm about to go before we start arguing about some shit that don't even exist."

"Yeah, you should go," she said slamming the door. As she peeped through the living room window, she noticed that Ivan reached into his pocket and pulled the white envelope out again and walked to the driver's window and handed it to him before walking to his door and hopping in the vehicle.

Weird. "Yes, this is Nyree Chandler. I'd like to report a burglary," she told the dispatch operator at the Gary Police Department.

IVAN MARRICK

Onyx drove the limo slowly out of Nyree's driveway. "So, how was your trip?" he inquired.

"Umm, ugh, I don't want to talk about it."

"So, it didn't go how you planned, huh, I told you about this chic," Onyx said as he drove past the lakefront.

"Yeah, I've got to step my game up. I fucked up when I took her to that club. I had too much to drink and was dancing with males and females in the club."

"Why… were… you… dancing… with… other… people? Why weren't you dancing with her?" Onyx asked sounding like a robot.

"She don't dance. In fact, she didn't even want to go to the club," Ivan recalled. After having said it aloud, he realized this is where he had gone wrong.

"You should have taken the romantic guy approach, I'm going to give you everything your ex couldn't give you approach. You would have won with that. This whole I'm a rich bad boy façade is failing you. I could tell she was annoyed with you when she got in the car."

"After all, I did to make the weekend perfect for her, and she acts like I'm just the average guy. Doesn't she know who I am and what I'm capable of doing?" Ivan fumed.

"No, she doesn't know how grimy you are. She doesn't know your past. You don't have a great reputation. You are trying to incorporate yourself into high society. So all that thug, criminal corruption street activity is not going to win her over. What you're going to do is be a compassionate guy. Find out what she likes and take an interest in it. You're not playing in the minor leagues anymore, and if you want to stay in the game, you're going to have to learn how to stay in the game. What was the purpose of having us break in her place and stealing that stuff? That was just plain dumb."

"I thought she would be afraid and want me to stay and comfort her. You got me out the spot, right?"

"Yeah, we got you a little low spot in Merrillville. However, it's not going to fit into the image you created for yourself. What are you going to do when she wants to come over?"

"I don't know. I'm hoping that by the time it gets serious she will just want me to move in with her. But I don't know because she's talking about having Malachi come stay with her until he gets better. Once again, he's created another problem for me."

"You could have let us kill him when we handled Rayna. We could've made it look like the crime of the century. I haven't heard that phrase since the whole O.J. and Nicole Brown- Simpson trial. O.J. was my dude. I can't believe he went and stole his items back. Dude's serving time like he killed somebody." Onyx laughed at his words. Ivan didn't see the humor in it until he thought about it again.

Ivan didn't really want to hear about how he should have handled Malachi. Was Malachi always going to be a thorn in his side, he wondered? Rubbing his hands together to create friction, he asked, "Were you able to transfer the money from her accounts to the other account?"

"Yeah, about that..."

"What you mean about that?" Ivan sensed that he was not going to like what was going to be said next.

Onyx looked into the rearview mirror and saw Ivan's face. "We couldn't do that. Do you know how much heat that would have put on you? She goes missing and during the first few days large sums of money are traced from her account to that W corporation account. You're asking for trouble."

"So, what am I going to do about money? I got a lifestyle."

"Well, when we went into Nyree's house we got a hold of some her personal information. I applied for some credit cards in her name and had them delivered to the new spot. All you got to do is buy some gift cards, get some cash advances, you know how we gets down," Onyx chuckled.

"Damn, Onyx."

"You hit that? She got you sprung?" Onyx inquired.

"Nah, nah, ain't nobody sprung." Ivan lied. The sex had been phenomenal. It had touched him on a deeper level. He wanted a family. Ivan had a dream that he was standing at the altar and Nyree was walking down the aisle.

"This is business. Remember you're getting back at Malachi for ruining your life. Nyree just happens to be a part of that. Don't get distracted. Remember the plan. Or we can see if we can do the department store thing again. You know, Petey still do the money thing in his basement, it's your call."

"Yeah, you right. Back to the plan. I guess we are going to have to do the department store thing. Get me a job working at one of those stores on U.S. 30. Give Petey some money to manufacture us some money. Get some of those chicks you know to come in there and buy some gift cards and we good. You know I can't do it that long, because if I get caught up. Nah, I'm not going to think negatively. I need money like yesterday. Man, just thinking about the operations reminds me of how me and Rayna used to get down back in the day. I will hold off on using those cards you got in chick's name until I have to use them. If she acts right, I should not have to, but the minute she start's acting funny style. Never mind all that. What's going on with your boy Colin Jordan?"

"He is willing to meet with you and help you with your Nyree situation. He's hoping you can convince her to speak on his behalf at his parole hearing. You all are on the same team. While he doesn't want her, he doesn't want to see her end up with Malachi. Y'all hate this dude, but I got to tell you, he's not that bad of a guy

126

which is why we went easy on him. He kept saying he had to stay alive for his wife and kids."

"Wife, who is he married to?" Ivan asked.

"Even though he's not married to Nyree; in his heart, that's always going to be his wife," Onyx announced as they pulled into the parking lot of an apartment complex in Merrillville, Indiana.

"Nah, Onyx, come on. This is where I'm going to be living? Seriously."

"Yeah, I know it's not your quarter of a million dollar home, but you got to stay low. You can't have anything associated with Rayna. The only way you were able to keep the Mercedes and Escalade is because those are in your mother's name. But it's good because you don't have a paper trail. It's like you don't exist. We got the furniture from the other spot, and this will feel like home. Got a storage unit in your mom's name too so, I will give you all the keys and paperwork for this stuff. By the way, how is your mom?

"Yeah, I got to call when I get settled," partially talking to Onyx and focusing himself on what needed to be done. He had spoken to Nick and Nick had stated that his mom was improving and had been sent back to the nursing home facility. Ivan sighed as he thought about the facility. That was another bill that would be coming due.

Ivan followed Onyx into the building, up the stairs and to apartment D. It was dreary and dank in the building. A myriad of smells. Somebody was cooking with too much garlic, and somebody had a whining baby. *Nah, this is not me. I got to go.* Opening the door to familiar items calmed Ivan's nerves a bit. This was not home, and he definitely was not trying to get acclimated. He had fallen in love with Nyree's home and could picture himself living there. Here in his very humble abode, he felt like a visitor. Onyx was giving him a tour and telling him about where his belongings were located. Ivan tried to listen, but he couldn't move past the fact that when Malachi broke it off with Rayna, he lost everything.

Onyx asked, "So, what do you think?"

"I think this shit is for the birds. This ain't me at all. You know how I get down. It's all good. I will bounce back from this. Tell me about Rayna and how it went down. No, never mind. I don't want to know."

Ivan rushed Onyx out of the apartment. He sat at his desk and contemplated how to win Nyree over.

NYREE CHANDLER

"Excuse me, ma'am, you can't just walk in there. I have a list of authorized persons, and I need to see identification," the thin security guard with the comb over Jheri curl told Nyree.

Nyree unzipped her leather jacket and stared at the man who was about two inches shorter than her. She knew exactly what his problem was, he had a Napolean complex, short man syndrome. Pulling out her wallet and retrieving her Indiana driver's license, she handed it to him, let him search her name and then she twisted her lips in expectation as she snatched her license back and put it back into the slot where she had previously removed it from in her wallet.

"I apologize," he said as he stared at the floor.

"Uh-huh," she dismissed him as she brushed past him and went inside the room. Malachi looked horrible she thought as she saw him hooked up to all the machines. Nyree had to fight back her tears as she eased into the recliner chair next to his bed. There were flowers, cards, and balloons all around the room. There was an outpouring of love from people. She felt herself on the verge of losing it. He needed her to be strong. If he were going to recover, everyone had to rally behind him and be strong. *I just might have to cut it off with IV. I can't even lie that was some good sex. That man got me feeling like I'm twenty-five. Ooh wee. Maybe it was because I haven't had sex in awhile. Lord, help me. Here I am sitting here at Malachi's hospital bed thinking about another man. Deliver me from temptation and evil. IV is something else.*

Malachi groaned and brought Nyree out of her thoughts. She turned her body to face him. He opened his eyes and squinted. "Is that m…m…my angel, Nyree, is that you for real?"

"Yes, it's me," she said as she allowed her hand to reach out and grab his hand. His grip was weak, but he held onto her tightly.

"I kn…kn..knew you w..w..would come. I knew India had her story w…w…wrong. She said something about you and a b…b…boyfriend. I kn…kn..knew that c…c…couldn't be. You s…saved my life. You w…w..were there with me, talking to me when they tried to kill me. You just kept encouraging me and telling me that I wasn't going to die. You believed when I didn't."

Unsure what to say, she nodded. Nyree wanted to say something to him about Ivan, but she didn't know what to say. This whole dating thing and seeing people was so strange to her. Was

Ivan her boyfriend? He was something to her. How would she introduce him? He was more than a friend, but was he her boyfriend? Titles and labels she could never seem to get them right.

"So, you want to tell me where you've been and what you've been up to? Oh and I'm sorry I missed your birthday. I promise I will make it up to you. I had plans for you but…" he laughed and continued, "shit happens. I got kidnapped in my own home. No, not kidnapped, what did the police call it…yeah, criminal confinement. Nyree, I'm only telling you this, but I felt helpless. Really, I really did. I've done some bogus, messed up type stuff and whew," he let out a breath and tears saturated his face. Nyree could tell he wanted to say more but was overcome with emotion. This was a totally different side of Malachi. He usually was so strong and macho and didn't show much emotion. He was emotional and vulnerable, and while she always wanted him to open up to her, this side of him made her uncomfortable.

She got up out of the chair and hugged him. When he released her, she looked out the window and commented, "Spring is here. It's six o'clock, and we still got signs of daylight. You look so uncomfortable. Can I get you something or do something?" Nyree wrinkled her nose.

"Yep and you can't say no or refuse. No excuses," he whispered and gave her a half-smile.

"You better not say anything nasty," she laughed.

"See…" he laughed for what seemed like an eternity and then he held his ribs in pain, "you're going to be the death of me. No, seriously, I want you to sing that song you always ask your grandma to sing."

"What song is that?" *I know he doesn't want me to sing a song for real. I heard he was on some real good drugs, but he's tripping for real. He's the one with the singing voice, not me.*

"Don't play with me, Girl. If you don't do it, I will call that guard in here and tell him you're abusing me."

"You wouldn't."

"Guard," he whispered. Getting louder, but still in a low tone," Guard." Clearing his throat he started but Nyree cut him off, "Okay. Okay. You know you're wrong don't you?"

Malachi didn't answer but just smiled in expectation.

Nyree crossed her arms around her body and closed her eyes.

"I've had some good days. I've had some hills to climb.

I've had some weary days and some lonely nights.

But when I look around, and I think things over.

You know what? All of my good days outweigh my bad days.

I won't complain."

"Sing Girl, sing Girl." Malachi encouraged her to continue. One of Nyree's gifts in life was that she had the gift of song.

"… so I will just say thank you, Lord. Thank you, Lord. God has been so good to me. He's been so good, he's been so good, he's been so good, whew…" Nyree fanned herself and hummed a bit … "I've been mistreated but thank you, Lord. I've been lied on but thank you, Lord. They broke in and stole my stuff, but I won't complain. They ransacked my home, but I just say thank you, Lord. I won't complain. I won't… I won't. " Nyree cried and wiped her eyes.

"Whoa, whoa Baby Girl, what do you mean they stole and ransacked your home? What are you talking about?"

Nyree sniffed and looked at him and just shook her head to indicate she didn't want to talk about it.

"So, you're keeping secrets from me?"

"There will be plenty of time to talk about that. I'm more concerned with you and who do you think did this to you?"

"Just what we've been trying to hammer out," a petite, muscular woman with a short pixie hair cut in a Hobart Police Department uniform said alongside a male police officer. The female officer continued, "So, you're Nyree Chandler?" she asked looking Nyree up and down. The officer looked liked she had just popped a lemon piece of candy into her mouth with the expectation it was something else. "We've been trying to get a hold of you, but it seems you've been out of town?"

"Yes. And why is that a concern?" Nyree was getting agitated. *Did this bitch just look me over like I wasn't nothing of importance?*

"Babe, calm down," Malachi interjected. Talking slowly with some mild stuttering he finally said, "They're just trying to figure out what happened? A lot of strange stuff has been happening. My incident. Rayna's missing, and then you said somebody broke into your house and ransacked it. I don't believe in coincidence."

The male officer spoke up, "Someone broke into your home, when? Did you report it?"

Nyree rolled her eyes. Why was everybody talking to her like she was mentally challenged? "I don't know when? When I was out of town. I reported it today to the Gary Police Department when I got home and noticed. You know what can we have this conversation elsewhere. I want Malachi to rest."

"Follow us," the male officer said as they walked toward the waiting area for guests.

It had been three weeks since Malachi had been discharged from the hospital and come home with Nyree and the children. The children were happy to have their dad in the house with them. Nyree marveled at how happy the children seemed to be. Although they were practically grown, having Malachi in the house seemed to make them happy. The children had told her that it would be great to have Malachi home with them. Nyree bought into the whole fairytale idea. It had been far from happily ever after. Her bedroom was upstairs and because Malachi didn't have the strength to make it up and downstairs his bedroom was the guest room on the lower level of the house.

Malachi was grouchy and withdrawn most days. His speech and processing were slow, and it was frustrating for Malachi which is why Nyree suspected that he had become withdrawn. Nyree had an interior decorator to come in and remodel the room. The first thing they did was to paint the room in hues of green with gold. The massage therapist from Chaotic Bliss said that this combination of colors would revitalize Malachi's mind. Nyree trusted the therapist but couldn't help but wonder when Malachi would come around. While she had always thought of him as a piece of work, to put it mildly, she would rather have the arrogant bastard around rather than this man who seemingly had given up on life. When the physical therapist visited for sessions, Malachi refused to participate in therapy sessions.

Popping her head into the doorway of the room, Nyree noticed Malachi lying in bed still as a board. She smiled hoping he might return the smile. "Hey Malachi," she said trying to bring him out of the trance he seemed to be in. "I'm going to stop by the office and the spa. Do you want anything?" she asked as she ran her fingers through her hair. She couldn't remember the last time she had been to the salon to have her hair done. Her fingernail got entangled in her hair. She felt tired. Looking at her hands, she quickly closed them. Her nails were an embarrassment. A manicure was in order, and she dreaded to think about her feet. Pedicure, had she had one this quarter? Damn and it was time to start thinking about taxes again. Tonight she would look over her financial statements. Generally, she did this monthly, but Nyree would be willing to bet she hadn't looked over these items since the end of February. While she paid an accountant to handle these things, she always wanted to make sure she was on top of things. For a brief moment, she remembered how Antoine Johnson had royally screwed her former best friend, Aris Smith over. Antoine had been her lover and accountant. Yeah, so he had literally fucked her, no pun intended.

"You look tired," Malachi told her. His statement brought her out of her thoughts.

"Well damn, thanks. I'm tired from being up with your ass all night. You can't sleep at night so instead of me sleeping in my bed, I'm down here sleeping in this chair. I'm up in the middle of the night helping you to the bathroom and who cooks for you when you're hungry at one in the morning? So, yeah it's hard for me to look all fabulous and shit when I'm doing domestic work." Nyree sauntered off and mumbled, "I didn't sign up for this shit. For real, for real."

These days she was using profanity more often to illustrate her points. A year ago, you would not have heard her talking like this. Now she cursed like a sailor and was up on all of the teen lingo. Last night she snapped chatted with a potential client. She was doing a lot of things that were out of character for her. Nyree was aware that she made the people around her uncomfortable with her new attitude and outlook on life. She was unapologetic about her behavior and didn't care who felt uneasy about her change. Perhaps that had been the problem, her whole life...she had been too concerned with what others thought and felt and neglected herself.

Walking down the hallway with her phone in hand and reading a text message she collided with the therapist in the hallway. "I apologize. I'm so busy reading this text and trying to get out of here. How are you today," she asked not really caring what his response would be.

"I'm good," he said, but there was something lingering in the air. Nyree sensed that he wanted to say more.

"Great and how is Malachi doing in his therapy? I've been meaning to contact you to ask you, but we seem to miss each other all the time. You're usually gone when I get back so I'm actually glad I bumped into you," Nyree laughed.

"Actually he's not doing anything. He's not trying at all. He simply refuses to comply with therapy."

Putting her phone in her handbag, she looked up at the therapist and asked, "So what do you do?"

He looked down at his gym shoes as though the answer were there. "I try to encourage him, but if he's not willing. I can't make him."

"I see. I get that. Yep, I truly get that. So, what is it that you do when he's uncooperative?"

"I document it and report it to the agency."

"Let me see if I have this correct. So, basically during the session, he's doing nothing, and you're documenting that he's doing nothing. In the meantime, I'm paying you one hundred- seventy dollars an hour to do nothing, correct?"

Nervously he spoke, "No, no. We have a program and regiment established and…"

"Okay, give me the treatment plan. He's going to complete it."

The therapist was on edge and ruffled through folders in his bag. He seemed relieved when he found the folder with Malachi's name on it. The moment he retrieved the treatment plan and put it in Nyree's hand a sense of calmness fell upon him. She snatched the papers from his hand and stormed down the hall toward her home gym with the therapist on her heels.

"Back already?" Malachi asked.

"I never left. I met your therapist in the hallway. What's this I'm hearing about you not doing what needs to be done in therapy?"

"Like you care," Malachi said boldy.

Nyree was shocked. It was the first time in weeks, Malachi had clearly articulated himself, and there was not a long pause.

"Say it again, if you dare."

"You heard me. Like you care," he repeated.

Nyree walked over to him and was in his personal space. "Okay, smart ass. This is how this is going to go. You're going to walk and dance like you've always done. I speak healing to your mind and body right now. You're going to follow this detailed treatment plan," Nyree told Malachi. Then she spun on her heel and turned to speak to the physical therapist. "Reggie? That's your name, right?"

"Yes," he said shoving his hands into the pants of his Nike warm up pants.

"You're fired. I don't need you standing here with your hands in your pockets doing nothing for one hundred seventy dollars an hour," Nyree told him as she began walking toward the door.

"You can't do that, Nyree" Malachi protested.

"Can and will. It's a done deal. Reggie, have a good day. I will see you out."

Malachi stood up and began taking steps toward Nyree. "I need Reggie to help me, " Malachi demanded.

"You do?" asked Nyree.

"I do," Malachi said firmly.

"He wants your help. I don't like you. I think you're a waste of time. So, I'm going to give you three more weeks. He has to walk into the children's graduation, with his cool walk, no cane, no walker. If he's not walking like I want him to be walking, you're out of here. Are you up for the challenge?"

"Yes ma'am," Reggie answered nervously.

"You know who I am right?" Nyree paused and watched Reggie nod his head to indicate he knew who she was. "Great. Your name will be ruined in this town and your agency as well if I make

138

my complaints public. I will have this same conversation with your supervisor," Nyree lowered her voice for impact.

Nyree ran over to Malachi and gave him a kiss on the cheek and smacked him on his behind. She was glad to see him acting more assertive. He was coming back around to being the Malachi she knew and loved. "Keep up the good work. Now, for real I am going to go see about our corporations."

He smiled. "What was that for? You look pretty."

Nyree said nothing. Instead, she put an extra sway in her hips as she left the room. She would bet all the money in her wallet that Malachi's eyes had been on her gluteus maximus as she exited the room.

IVAN MARRICK

It had been four weeks since Ivan had seen Nyree. They had talked for hours and hours. Some people had gone to work and gotten off work during the time they had been on the phone. Then there had been the video chats. Ivan smiled as he recalled their last conversation as he stood at Nyree's front door. "You know I used to be a stripper," he had lied.

Nyree laughed, "Oh really?"

"Yeah, really, I ain't lying," he lied again.

"Well, then let me see some of your moves."

"Okay, not a problem," he told her as he began to disrobe and engage in acts on video chat that would make a porn star blush.

"Now, your turn," he told her.

She stuck her tongue out in a provoking manner, "Nah, I'm good."

"Yes, you are, but let me see a little something, something. You're shaking your head, no. Well, at least send me a pic."

"Okay, did you get it? I just sent it."

Ivan fell out on the floor laughing uncontrollably. "Are you serious? Nah, you can't be. You just sent me this PG picture. Get the hell out of here. What, you don't trust me?"

Nyree had gotten quiet. She usually had a lot to say, but that question had shut her down.

"Really? Okay, you know what. I'm going to go, and I'll get at you."

After what seemed like an eternity, the door finally opened. "Hey, Sweetie. I'm back. Did you miss me?" Ivan asked as Nyree stared at him in amazement.

"Um, yeah," she hesitated. Clearly, she was caught off guard by his presence at her home. Opening the door wider, she motioned for him to come in and said, "Come on in. We're going to be in the living room," she told him sounding very formal. As they walked through the foyer and into the living room, Ivan looked around, and things were different. Furniture had been rearranged. There were alarm sensors throughout the room and a view of cameras visible to the site. If he could see them, then that meant there were several hidden. This knowledge had been obtained from when he used to install security equipment for a local alarm company. It had been easy to compromise Nyree's system over a month ago when they were in Orlando because he was the person who installed her equipment years ago. He infiltrated her system the day they left for Orlando. He arrived earlier than he told her he would be arriving to pick her up. "Just make yourself at home," she had hollered. Following her directions, he did just that and deactivated monitors. Those rooms gave access to Onyx's team without tripping the system.

Sitting down on the new Italian leather sofa, he commented, "I see you got cameras all up in this motherf…my bad." He told her as her look suggested that he should not use that profane word in her home.

"Yeah, yeah. We upgraded the system. It's crazy, you would have thought that they guy who installed the equipment would have suggested that I purchased more equipment for this fifty-five hundred square foot house. Um, a lot of crazy stuff has happened since we've been going out."

"Nyree, is that my nurse?" Malachi's voice called from a distance, but every word he spoke seemed he was getting closer to the living room, "Have you seen my…" Malachi paused as he slowly walked into the living room and saw Nyree and Ivan sitting on the sofa next to each other.

"Have I seen your what?" Nyree asked giving her full attention to Malachi as she stood up.

"Never mind. I didn't realize you had a visitor," Malachi stood in the doorway looking disappointed.

Nyree let out a sigh. "Yes, this is Ivan Marrick. Ivan Marrick this is Malachi Chandler."

Ivan stood and walked to Malachi, "Yeah, good seeing you again," and extended his hand.

Malachi didn't extend his hand, and Ivan quickly brought his hand to his side. Malachi looked puzzled. "Again?"

Nyree chimed in, "Sure, you've met. He's on your VIP list at the spa."

"Hmm. Interesting. And you're here to see Nyree about spa business?"

"No, not at all," Ivan laughed, "this is a social call. I'm trying to change her last name. But as for today I just want her to go wine tasting with me at Anderson's Winery in Valparaiso. I just got back in town from Atlanta. I was down there checking on my music group, "Cadence" and…"

"Cadence is your music group?" Malachi asked astonished.

Nyree wrinkled her nose at Ivan and then drew her attention to Malachi. She stared at Ivan who seemed very preoccupied with his cell phone. Clearing her throat, she asked, "Is everything okay, IV?"

He continued tapping on his screen and didn't respond. After three more taps and a couple of swipes to his phone he sent https://soundcloud.com/jerome-goldenschwartze/50-shades-of-gold-mastered to her phone. "Yeah, the engineer just sent the mastered version of 50 Shades of Gold to me. I just sent it to your phone."

"Okay, cool, I can't wait to hear it. I just heard the notification go off on my phone. Dang, where did I leave my phone?

"You left it in my room earlier. I'm going to go lie down. Do you want me to bring it to you or are you going to come get it," he winked as he began walking away toward his room.

Clearing his throat, Ivan said, "Take care. Nice seeing you again." Sitting down on the sofa and encouraging her to sit with him, Ivan told Nyree, "I will play the song for you on my phone. So, you were in his room, huh," Ivan pretended to be jealous.

"Anyways," Nyree said not offering much more conversation on the subject.

"Anyways, that's all you going to say," he smiled and then leaned in and planted a kiss on her lips.

"It's been a long time no see, Mr. Marrick. How come I didn't know you were in Atlanta. You said you were in Indianapolis?"

"Yes, I was in Nap and then went to check on my properties and my music group. I told you about my record company down in Atlanta. While I was down there, I was in the studio and decided to lay down that track for you. Shh, listen and tell me what you think."

"Oh, my gosh, that was fantastic, IV," she hugged him tightly.

"Wow, if you liked that, then I know you're going to love this," he reached into his front pocket and pulled out a five karat yellow diamond ring and slipped it on his pinky finger, "what would you do if I put this on your finger?"

Clearly, he had caught Nyree off guard. Her eyes widened. "Put it on there and find out," Nyree dared him.

"See, you're playing, and I want that 'til death do us part. You thought I was playing when I told Malachi that I want to change your last name. I'm not playing. You know what? This house is way too small for us. I say let's go house shopping and get something bigger. I can have my company build one or you know what might be fun… since you own a construction and development company. It would be good if my company collaborated with your company and we build something together. That's what I'm on building a future. You're up here playing house with your ex and think I'm supposed to be okay with this shit. Nah, you know what you playing childish games. You need to grow up. I'm trying to take you to another level, and you just want to stay in your little comfort zone with Malachi."

"Mom, you know prom is in about two weeks. I got to go get a tux and all kinds of stuff," Christian burst into the living room frantically.

"Calm down Christian, you said you were not going to do prom. You weren't going to conform to everyone's expectations and traditions and something else, so why the change of heart now?"

"I've got to be there. I want to go. Bianca wants to go and…"

"Hey, Chris, I can take you to look for tuxes and all of that since your mom does not want to go out today."

"What Ivan? You know what, we will finish that discussion later. You don't have to take Christian to look for a tux that won't be necessary."

"Yeah, he has his parents here. We got this. Maybe you should stick to your music group and your properties, and I will manage my family," Malachi said. Everyone was staring at him in amazement as no one had even heard him slip back into the room.

"My fault Man, I didn't mean to offend you. I know you've been out of sorts lately, and I was just trying to make sure Christian was straight, but by all means do your thing. I didn't mean to step on your toes."

"Yep."

"Well, I guess I will be leaving," Ivan said getting up. He looks disappointed that Nyree didn't discourage him from leaving.

Nyree took Ivan's hand and began walking with him to the foyer. "Call me later. We really need to talk."

"I don't think so. You just want to play with my heart like it's a game. I'm not a toy to be played with. I was trying to have something serious with you, but you've made your choice. One day you're going to be sorry. You're going to wake up, and your life is going to be out of sorts."

"Don't fucking threaten me, IV," Nyree leaned in toward him and whispered.

The front door opened widely, and India fell into Ivan who caught her.

"Hey, My Angel, how are you?"

"Ivan!!!! Oh my gosh, I haven't seen you since Cain killed Abel," she hugged him as if he were her best friend in the world.

"Ah, My Angel, I'm glad somebody around here appreciates me. And how did you do on your exam in Calculus."

" I aced it of course. Thanks so much. I did what you said, and I got it."

"What's going on here?" Nyree inquired.

"Oh, India was having some problems with Calculus, and so she texted me, and I showed her how to solve these equations. You probably would know this if you weren't so into yourself and your corporations. Your daughter was on the verge of failing and reached out to me."

"India?" Nyree demanded.

"Mom, you're no good at math, so I remember Ivan saying he was great in math when he was in school and he helped me. Geez, it's not that big of a deal. I'm not going to fail. You should be thanking Ivan instead of having an attitude."

"India, I don't know what has gotten into you, but you better check that attitude at the door."

"Don't yell at My Angel. Look India, I brought you something from my travels," he told her as he reached into his pocket and pulled out a tear drop pendant filled with over ninety-one diamond stones.

"She can't accept that." Nyree rolled her eyes and put her hands on her hips.

"Nyree, don't. It can be an early graduation gift," he turned and left the house.

Ivan put his black Camaro in reverse and sped down Nyree's street, as he came upon the curve he finally decided to put his foot on the brake. There were some many twists and turns in the Miller section of Gary. He would kill himself if he continued at that speed. "Call Onyx," he commanded his car.

"What's up, IV?" Onyx asked.

"I tried. I tried. These women don't want anyone who is going to treat them right. They want a dog and then when they get that they complain. I told her we should be a family, get a house together, showed her the ring and she looked at me like I had the plague. That's not what she wants. She wants to play house with her ex."

"And this is what she said?" Onyx inquired.

"No, she didn't have to say it. She looked at me like I was nothing. So we go forth with Operation Charity. I want you to apply for every line of credit you can get in her name. I am not used to living like this."

"IV, I don't know. Isn't this risky? I mean we just got you a 2017 Camaro in her name. What happened with the check? Did Nyree take it?"

"Hell naw, she didn't take it. She didn't even think twice about it. She told me to cash it and give her the money or keep it."

"The check was for fifteen thousand dollars…"

"I know that Onyx, I'm the one who wrote it out. I guess I will push it through. It's from a checkbook I stole years ago. Chick had a lot of money. I always said I would use it on a rainy day. I'm not quite ready to use it."

"You're one cold-hearted son-of-a-bitch. You're going to ruin your momma's good name and credit and this chick you used to date and Nyree? Think about this; your momma, Man?"

"My momma is not getting better. I met with the doctor, and he said I need to really take her off of life support. She cannot function without the life support and look, that money from the Dub Mart operation is not going to last forever. I'm going to have to make a decision real soon about my mom and her greedy ass brother keep's calling wanting to know what's going on. He thinks she is leaving him some money in the will. Her will is under lock and key with Attorney Shauna Buchanan. You know that's one tough cookie. That's the one that had the baby by that one mayor, and his wife tried to kill her. That heifer is still doing time, and I know that had to have been at least ten years ago."

"Damn dude. You always manage to be at the center of some drama. I was just thinking the other day. I think I want to clean my life up. I'm tired of doing dirt. The reason I can't sleep at night is because I am haunted by all the wicked shit I've done in my life. I'm tired of going to sleep when the sun rises. Do you know the torment I endure? Real shit, I'm going to help you out with this episode and then it's my season finale. I'm done."

Ivan pulled into the parking lot of his complex. Snatched the key out of the ignition. "Nope Onyx, you're done when I say you're done. But I hear you. Once I get my hands on the money my momma left me in the will, I'm done. She always used to say that there was money from the sale of the nightclub my grand-daddy owned and that she had put it in her will for me. She said real parents leave their children an inheritance."

"So, you're literally banking on your momma's death to make you rich?"

"Yep! You know what, I got to get off of here. I am going to go see about cashing that check," Ivan told Onyx. He reached into his glove compartment and retrieved four blank checks with Malachi Chandler's name on them. *It's about time I showed this dude who he's messing with.*

Ivan drove over to the PLS Check Cashing Center on 7th and Broadway in Gary. He was a little nervous about making the transaction, but the adrenaline rush he was experiencing was better than any drug high he had encountered previously.

"Good afternoon, that periwinkle blue is very flattering on you," he told the cashier as he pushed the check toward her along with his identification.

"Thank you. Is this Malachi Chandler the rapper?"

"Shh, you know this is supposed to be low key. He does not like people knowing who his staff members are? You know with all he's going through, so can I count on you being discreet."

"Yeah, of course. I just have to call his bank and verify it."

Ivan chuckled, "Really? You know this little bitty check, he's good for it. I mean everybody in America who works has this in their checking account. This is petty cash," Ivan teased.

"Nope, I wish I had this lying in my bank account. I guess I'm the working class because we call six thousand dollars bill money."

"You got a man?" Ivan asked.

"No, why?"

"We could talk about it tonight over dinner. Sweetie, cash that out. Give me your number and let's go to the Cheesecake Factory tonight."

"Okay, I'm Tianna," the young cashier told Ivan as she counted out the money in various denominations. After handing Ivan the money, she gave Ivan her phone number so he could program it into his phone. He logged her into his contacts as $$$Chick.

"I will give you a call later. What time do you get off?"

"I get off at seven."

"Cool, text me your address and I will pick you up around eight-thirty. Then we will drive out the John Hancock Center in

Chicago and have dinner at the Cheesecake Factory unless you prefer the one in Orland Park?"

"No, the one in the Hancock Center is fine," the twenty-something young woman with curly weave hanging down the middle of her back told Ivan. She was not his type at all. Too much make-up and clearly overly excited about a man who had material things. The one thing that worked in his favor was that she could be controlled. She hadn't followed the protocol of the currency exchange which meant that he should be able to cash the other three checks without a problem.

Ivan hurried to his car and sent Nyree a text. *So, you think you can just play with someone's emotions. You're used to stringing people along and playing games with them. Well, you picked the wrong one this time. I'm going to turn your little world upside down.*

Ivan, what are you talking about? Nobody played with your emotions.

Nyree, you're going to get what's coming to you. You're used to taking and taking. This time, you're going to give. It would be a shame if those pics you sexted me went public. I'm sure the university wouldn't want to have a guest professor on staff who posts pics on porn sites.

Ivan, why are you doing this?

Nyree, why not? Those pics will be leaked if I don't get what I want.

What do you want, Ivan?

I will let you know, Sweetie, be prepared to pay and as you know I do everything big!

MALACHI CHANDLER

As soon as Nyree pulled up into the driveway and put the vehicle into park, Malachi eased out of the front seat of the truck and walked to the front door of Nyree's home without incident. It felt good to be out and about. While he was not operating at one hundred percent capacity, he was getting there.

"Let's watch a movie," Malachi suggested as he positioned himself comfortably on the sofa when Nyree finally made her way into the living room.

"Um, I don't know. I was thinking I would lie down. You know I'm not really feeling well."

"What? We just left the kids' grand march. Didn't they look great with their prom dates? You seemed to be okay when we were at the school. I'm not trying to be in your business, but I will tell you, you haven't been yourself since that day Ivan Marrick was here? Did you all have a fight?" Malachi bombarded her with a barrage of questions.

"Okay, what is this twenty questions? Christian and India looked great. I don't know if I like that boy she's going out with. I am glad that she and Christian are double dating. I haven't been feeling well all week if the truth be told. You think I'm upset over a guy. Come on Malachi. We had an argument, but it's nothing."

"Really, because I thought I heard him yelling at you, but I know you're a big girl and can take care of yourself, but you seem different."

"I don't want to talk about it." She shrugged her shoulders and started fidgeting with her earrings. Earlier in the day she and Malachi had been crawling around on the living room floor looking for the two-karat diamond stud.

"Okay, you don't have to talk. I'm going to talk. Ever since this guy came into your life, some crazy shit has been happening. Then the other day we out having breakfast, this dude calls you and what do you do, you bring me home and rush off to meet him. That was real messed up. Yep, you've done some classic foul stuff, and that is probably at the top of the list."

"So since we are talking about it, Malachi. I apologize. Just like I don't discuss you with IV, I don't discuss his personal stuff with you, but since you must know and maybe this will keep you from speculating or supposing that you know what is going on…his mother is battling cancer. The doctors had her on life support and said that there was nothing else that could be done for her. He made the decision to take her off, and he just needed someone to be there with him when it happened."

"I feel bad for dude and his moms and all, but you mean to tell me he didn't have any family he could have called?"

"His uncle was in town from Tennessee but left last week. I don't know how would feel or act if I had the weight of the world on my shoulders. Before you're so quick to judge, remember your family didn't really show up for you when you were in the hospital."

"You are my family," he reached out and grabbed her hand, "I don't care if you get married again, I'm always going to see you as my wife. My love for you is so…"

"Oh, somebody took their meds today," Nyree teased.

"I'm trying to be serious with you, Nyree, and you want to make a joke. Who's blowing your phone up? I bet that's your little boyfriend."

Nyree looked down at her phone and smiled at Malachi. His phone notifications for texts started going off one and after another. "Your little girlfriend," she laughed as she looked at the texts.

"These kids going to blow my phone up with these pics. Did you know anything about them staying at the Embassy Suites tonight?"

"What are you talking about?" Nyree jumped up. "Come on. We are going up to that prom. There is not going to be any Embassy Suites on my watch. And you act like you're okay with this. Why are you still sitting there? Bring your tail," Nyree told him as she stood at the door with her purse on her shoulder.

"Oh my goodness. You should see yourself," he told her as he ended the video of her. He imitated her voice, "Ain't gonna be no Embassy Suites on my watch. And so, you're okay with this? Why are you still sitting there?" Malachi laughed until he cried. Gasping for air, "Oooh, I got you and I got you good and everybody on Facebook bout to see it. This is payback for how you got me last year. Oh, my, you don't know how long I've been waiting for this moment."

"Ugh, I can't stand you. You get on the nerve before my last nerve," she pouted as she put her purse down and set the alarm. "I swear, you make me sick. I'm going to make some pasta, you want some."

"Yeah. Hell yeah, I'm hungry as a hostage," Malachi rubbed his belly.

"Okay, well come in the kitchen and keep me company."

As Malachi settled on the stool at the breakfast nook, he shared with Nyree, "You know this reminds me of the time I cooked for you years ago on your birthday. It was the first time you had been to my house on Lakeshore Drive. Do you remember that?"

"Yeah, I remember that," she smiled, "India was in the hospital sick. That girl is a fighter. She was in the fight for her life, but she made it. Look at her now. Life was hectic then, but it was simpler then, wouldn't you say?"

"We've always gotten through our troubles. It's like we manage to find bliss in the midst of our chaos. Why do you think I named the spa, Chaotic Bliss? I only bought that place so that you would have a place of your own to experience bliss in the midst of all the chaotic shit in the world."

Nyree smiled as she chopped up onions and green peppers. "Who are you? You talk about me being different? You're different. I would have never expected you to say that."

"No, no, I'm Malachi. I'm that dude. I'm that dude that you love and who gets next to your last nerve. It's so much I've wanted to say to you for years, but my pride got in the way, and then I got distracted with Rayna," he paused and looked down.

"You love her still. I'm sorry about her. I mean I never liked her, but I pray at night that she will be found safe and sound. And you have got to know I didn't have anything with her going missing."

"I did love her. I was settling for second best. I wanted you. She tried to do everything to make me happy, and I know that, but she wasn't you. I told her I couldn't do it no more. Anyway enough about her money hungry self. See that's what doesn't make sense. As much as she likes money and revenge she just disappears without a trace. Nobody has heard from her?"

"You think she's dead?" Nyree asked as she began sautéing the shrimp, chicken, and mushrooms.

Malachi reached over into the frying pan and swiped a piece of chicken and put it into his mouth. "This is pretty good. Even though you don't season your meat like black people do, this is still good."

"What?" Nyree burst into laughter, "I don't season my food like black people. That's crazy. I mean if you're saying I don't dump half a bottle of seasoning salt and other spices on my food like you do, then I guess you're right. You have got to watch your salt intake and stop eating half done chicken, you'll get salmonella poisoning. I've been saying this to you over twenty years now. You conveniently didn't answer me about Rayna. Do you thinks she's dead?"

Malachi rubbed his cupped his temples and allowed his hand to slowly drag down his face, he sighed, "Yeah, I think she may have met her demise. Now who and why?"

"Who and why?" Nyree asked loudly, "The woman had enemies. She pissed a lot of people off with interviews and statements she has made over the years. I was so glad when I got back from Orlando she was not up in my face with a camera asking me about you. I think I would have Molly Whopped her tail this time."

"You know what?" He laughed as he asked the question, "Every time I think I'm real certain about you and I know you, you go and say something that makes me question how well I know you. Check that pasta. Don't nobody want mashed potatoes for penne? Have you even ever been in a fight? You talking about Molly Whopping somebody. Real talk don't be around talking like that. It makes you look suspect."

"Hello," Nyree said after trying to figure who could be calling from the 1-800 number that flashed across her screen. "This is she. What? I haven't been to the Chanel store on North Michigan. Am I sure? Um, yes, I don't carry Chanel. Which card did you say this was...my Black card? See I know this is not a real call. You all don't even call it the Black card anymore, it's Centurion. This is not American Express. Visa Black? I don't have a Visa Black. Do I want to speak to the fraud department? That's cute when you're perpetrating a fraud. If I don't believe you're a real representative I can call back and ask about claim number, wait, let me write this down." She scribbled the information down and put the paper off to the side.

"What's up, Babe?"

"This is the second time this week somebody has called me about a credit card and excessive activity. It's always with a card I don't have. Then I saw some mail from credit card people, but I didn't open it up. I've been meaning to, but I just thought it was junk mail. Let me rinse this pasta off."

"Is everything okay with your finances? I've been meaning to ask you about..." he trailed because he wanted to be careful regarding how he worded what he wanted to say.

"About what?" she asked as she nibbled on a piece of shrimp. Walking over to the freezer she pulled out a loaf of garlic bread and placed it on the cooking workstation. She skipped over to the sink and washed her hands. "Can you hand me a cutting board? Now you were saying," she asked as she took the cutting board from Malachi and placed the bread on it and began to slice it into sections.

Malachi watched her as she lightly sprayed the tin pan and put the bread on it. He smiled as he watched her bend over and place the pan in the oven. "Yeah, you've been writing quite a few checks on my account and I'm not tripping because I know you've been paying bills, but I don't usually spend twenty-four thousand dollars in a month."

"What? What are you talking about? Twenty-four thousand dollars? I don't spend like that. Why are you saying I did that?"

"I mean I can see the checks online. You made them out to yourself and cashed them. Each one has been for six thousand dollars. I mean and it's cool if you needed money to pay for my expenses, but it just seems excessive in the past month."

"Um, I don't know what to say. I didn't do that."

Malachi picked up his phone and logged into his online banking application and showed Nyree the checks he was making reference to. She shook her head as she saw these checks were endorsed to her and then she looked at the signature on the back of the checks and hollered.

"That's not my signature. You know my signature. Who in the hell did this? I know…"

"You know who did this?" Malachi pounded his fist on the table.

"Grab the plates and silverware. You want wine?" Nyree asked.

Setting the table, Malachi yelled, "Wine is good. But I asked you a question, who did this and you knew about it?"

"No, I don't know who did this. I was going to say I know Ivan didn't do this."

"Why would you think your little boyfriend did this? Speaking of him, I don't have a good feeling about him. There is something not right with that dude. I'm telling you he ain't right Nyree. I'm not homophobic, but I don't think he's totally into women."

"Malachi, what?"

"Real talk. I pick up a vibe from him that he's not totally into women. But back to you thinking he stole my money. I will twist his cap back."

Pouring wine into their glasses, as they sat at the kitchen table, Nyree said, "Hmm."

Impatiently Malachi asked, "Hmm what? Look like you day-dreaming. Tell me something, Nyree."

"He has been threatening me. Sending me texts telling me he was going to ruin my name and that when it was over, I would be going on a long trip away from the family. He said you were going to pay for all the stuff you've taken from people. It just seems like in the wake of those threats. No, he would not do that. How would he get your checks? When we finish eating, I'm going to call that credit card company back and look at that mail."

"Nyree this doesn't make sense. It's something you not telling me," Malachi winced in pain.

"Are you okay? Do you want a pain pill?"

"I'm in a little pain, but no, I can't have wine and medicine. Besides, I need to be alert. We got a problem. How did he get my checks? Do you remember when I was attacked in my home?"

"Yes, I remember, and you do know me and him were in Orlando."

"This is very weird to me. How long did you know him before you went traipsing off with him? He telling me he's VIP at Chaotic Bliss. That's strange. I know all the VIPS by name and face. I had never seen him a day in my life. You know what… Maybe I have seen him. It's been years, though. I used to serve his father when I was in the dope game. That silly motherfu…dude had everything, but drugs took his life over. Kind of sad."

"Really Malachi, now you're the poster boy for "Say No To Drugs." You know when we were in Orlando we went to this club, and he was dancing with dudes. I mean it was some bizarre stuff I've never seen in my life."

"Um. But you never said how long you've known him. What do you know about him? Where does he stay?"

"He's part owner of that new club in Midtown, owns a gas station on the west side and he's got his music company that's based in Atlanta."

"He is not part owner of that new club in Midtown. That's my boy's club." Malachi dialed his friend on the phone and put it on speaker phone. "Hey Man, what's up with you? Just wanted to ask you how things were going with the club and see if you and your partner, Ivan Marrick needed anything?"

"It's all good, Malachi. Maybe when you feeling up to it, you can come do a concert. What you mean my partner, Ivan Marrick?" Jeremy Collins asked.

"For sure, I can do a concert. Word on the street is that Ivan Marrick is your partner in the club."

"Nope. I know that fool is not out there telling people that. His company started doing the construction on the club but didn't finish. He stole about thirty thousand dollars from me. I bet not see him in these streets."

"Stole thirty G's from you? What you mean?" Malachi asked as he looked at Nyree.

"I paid him for materials and labor up front. He never finished. He said somebody stole the material. When I asked for the receipts for the materials so I could submit a claim to the insurance company. He couldn't produce them. Phone got disconnected. I tried to file a claim with the Better Business Bureau, come to find out his company didn't even exist."

"Didn't exist?"

"Yeah, didn't exist. I thought he was legit because back in the day his daddy was the man in the city along with your wife's dad with the construction in Gary. And Ivan and his crew did some work, and it was solid, but Malachi, I had to have somebody come finish the job, and I'm out of thirty thousand dollars. I filed a police report, but nothing has ever come of it. The police say because I didn't have a contract and it was just two men's word it will be hard to take action."

"Damn, Dawg, that's messed up."

"Exactly, but Karma is not kind, and Ivan Marrick is going to get his. Let me get off of here. We're getting ready to open up in a few minutes."

"Alright."

"Alright. Stay up," Jeremy told Malachi before hanging up.

"So, what you think?" Malachi asked Nyree as he chewed on his bread.

"How would he have gotten your checks?" Nyree asked.

"Who could have gotten a hold to your information to open these credit cards in your name? As you can see this is not junk mail."

"I'm sick," Nyree told Malachi as she placed the dishes in the dishwasher.

Malachi grabbed Nyree by the arms and spun her around to him. "No, you're not sick. This is no time for you to go getting weak. We always come out on top. I was down for the count for a minute, and you held it down. I need you to stay strong. I'm almost fully back. This motherfucker, excuse my language, but he picked the wrong family to mess with."

"We don't know that it's him. We can't go around accusing people."

"You're right. We can't go around pointing fingers at people, so I'm pointing him out. But you know what, come on in the living room. Let's put our movie on and I will tell you how we're going to play this out and he's going to get himself caught up."

"You don't think it's any of the staff?"

"Nyree, no. No, I don't. We've had these staff members forever and a day and we've never, did I say never, never had a problem with any of our staff members. Now, here is what I know. This petty criminal comes around seven months ago, and now we got problems we've never had before. He's taking his criminal activity to another level."

"What do you mean criminal activity?"

"I did a background check on him. He's got DUIs, suspended license, evictions, and even owes the funeral home for his grandmother's funeral. Yeah, I had to check him out. He's a liar. I knew that from the day he told us that Cadence was his group. You know that's my group. He's the type that lies for no reason. Tries to impress people. But that one lie made me question his whole being. Rest your head on my chest. You don't have to be nervous, anxious nothing. I got you. Here's your phone back. I'm going to stop reading these texts because I will go to that hospital and wait for him to show up and then…"

"Malachi, stop."

"I'm getting a little tired and stiff. Put the alarm on. I'm going to go get in the bed. Don't look like that. You can always come with me," he smiled.

"You know what?"

"Tell me."

"I think I will come hang out in your room."

"That's what's up," Malachi smiled trying to remember the last time he had sex. He quickly stopped himself from going back down memory lane. He didn't want to think about Rayna and that's where that memory was going to take him.

"We should take a nap so we will be well rested when the kids get here, and we can hear all about their night. You know we have to go down to the police station tomorrow morning."

Nyree said nothing, but she nodded her head as she sat on the edge of the bed. Malachi handed her the remote control and told her to find something for them to watch on television. They both knew they would be sleep within minutes. This had always been their bedtime ritual. She was in charge of finding something on television for them to watch until they fell asleep. Finally, her search ceased when she saw Kevin James and Leah Remini in one of her favorite sitcoms, "The King of Queens."

Malachi turned his back to Nyree who was propped up in the bed. He pretended to be asleep. He was waiting for Nyree to fall asleep. She was a heavy sleeper. When she fell asleep, he would slip into the den and get on his computer and see if Amber Shaw of Dilworth Detective Agency had emailed him any findings on Ivan Marrick. For a brief moment in time, Amber had been married to Edwin Shaw, Nyree's father before he passed. Amber was a great investigator. Malachi recalled just how good Amber was at her job. She had been the one hired by Edwin when he was still married to Margo, Nyree's mother to dig up information on Margo. Malachi couldn't prove it yet, but he was sure that Ivan was behind this mess. He kept replaying what Jeremy Collins said and then even what Rayna said the night he broke up with her. Her voice hadn't been loud, but it had been forceful when she said, "Malachi, you're definitely going to pay in more ways than one." *It seems like I haven't stopped paying since that night.*

NYREE CHANDLER

Nyree rolled over on her side and opened her eyes, she was surprised to find that she was not on the sofa in the living room. *Where in the world am I? I slept in my clothes. What happened last night for me to end up in Malachi's bed? We had dinner and too much wine. We didn't have sex, I would have remembered that or would I? I'm beyond tired.*

Nyree heard laughter coming from the living room. It was Malachi and the children. The door chime alerted her that the front door was open. "Be safe and enjoy yourself," he heard Malachi instructing the children.

"Malachi. MALACHI!" Nyree yelled.

He strolled into the room with a breakfast tray. Malachi was doing well holding the tray and walking with it. Nyree was proud to see the progress. She wondered if he may be overdoing it, though.

"Ah, a beautiful woman in my bed yelling my name what more could I ask for?" He smiled as he gently sat the tray on her lap. "Breakfast for you. Happy Mother's Day. I know I'm early, but you deserve it. You have really held this family down this year. The kids are gone to Six Flags. What's that look?"

"Nothing, I was just thinking."

"Umph, tell me," he told her as he stole a piece of bacon off her plate.

She smacked his hand. "You know I hate when you dig into my plate. Did you cook a whole pack of bacon?" she asked as she looked at the pile of bacon on her plate.

"I cooked enough for the two of us."

"Ah, I knew there was a catch to this."

"Don't act like I've made breakfast in bed for you. And I did the Mickey Mouse pancakes too."

"Yes, I remember. You smell so good," she told him as she gazed into his coffee with cream eyes.

"Thank you, hun. You know when you finish eating we have to go to the Police station."

"Yep," Nyree said sullenly.

"You don't sound like you want to go. We talked about our plan last night, Nyree. We have to take our lives back. I'm not going to let that light bright looking motherfu… umm," he paused and took a deep breath. Nyree could tell he was getting worked up. "He's not going to ruin our lives. I promise you that. I'm getting stronger each and every day. I'm sorry you had to take care of me, but I appreciate you being there for me. I don't think I've ever told you that. Now, I'm stepping up and being here for you. I think you ended up with him because you were looking for something and you thought the answer was with him. No, the answer is between you and I, Nyree. You know that. You've known that since day one when we met. I got under your skin. I was like no other guy you had met. I still get under your skin, and you love that I'm like no other guy you've met," Malachi told Nyree as he swiped another slice of bacon and chewed it.

"Ugh!!! Would you stop! I'm going to beat your tail, Malachi. You're definitely one of a kind. I don't know if we can be a "we." How many times have we done that dance?"

"Look, let's not focus on what went wrong. Let's figure out how to get our lives back on track. I got to go home."

Nyree looked sad when he said those words about going home. "Why? I thought you liked being here with us," she told him as she straightened the bed and watched him recline in the leather recliner.

"I love being here with you all. I just need to see the scene of the crime. I can't keep avoiding it. Now, if we're talking long term that goes back to me wanting "us" but you just said you didn't want that." Malachi shrugged his shoulders as if he were confused.

"Alright, Malachi let's do this" Nyree sat down on the bed and motioned for him to come sit next to her. When he made his way to her side she spoke from the heart, "Alright, I tried to table this discussion, but since you brought it up again, let's deal with the elephant in the room. Let's have this conversation. For years, I held out, put my life on hold, didn't date or get in a serious relationship because I thought we would get back together. I thought it would be an "us" a "we." You, on the other hand, wanted your cake, ice cream, and pie. Then you went and got involved with Rayna, yet you were still coming over here hanging out, taking me out, but going home to her. So, I came to myself and said you couldn't keep dipping in and out of my pie without a commitment. So, even when we stopped having sex, you continued to do bae stuff, you would come and take my truck and fill it up. You made sure it made it to every maintenance appointment. We still went to movies and concerts, but there was no commitment. I'm forty-five and my next breath ain't promised, but I want to spend my last days with someone who is committed to me. And if you can't honestly be that person then shut the fuck up, real talk."

Nyree got up to walk out the room. Malachi caught her by the arm. "Oh hell nah, it's my turn now. You don't get to say all that and walk off. Is that what these little young whippersnappers let you do? You're dealing with a real man. I don't care about you rolling your eyes. I'm supposed to be scared. You're so funny," he told her as she wrinkled her nose. He squeezed her nose. Neither one of them were sure why he did it, but it was a gesture he had been doing for over twenty years especially when she made the face that she had just made. "Okay, I love you. I always have. Does that mean, I haven't messed up or hurt you? The answer is no. Am I sorry for what I have done? More than I can tell you. I am so sorry for the mess I've put you through over the years. You said earlier that we've done this dance too many times. You're right. I want this to be our last time doing it. I promise you I just want us. I think you want the same thing too. I know I hurt you before. That's in the past. I told Rayna it was over with us the night before this crazy ordeal unfolded."

"What?" Nyree questioned.

"I broke up with Rayna the night before. I was going to discuss this with you on the day it went down, but I never made it out the house."

"How come I never knew this?"

"It has been hard for me to open up. The therapy sessions have really been helping me. I felt so vulnerable and weak, and I thought you just had me here because you felt sorry for me. Doc told me that I had to open up and tell you how I felt. I was so angry and bitter when I saw you and Ivan sitting on the couch. I was like, that's supposed to be me. Doc told me it was my responsibility to let you know how I felt about you. He said if I laid up in this room and let somebody come in here and snatch you up, then the only person I could blame would be me."

"Wow," Nyree said.

"I know you're not speechless," Malachi snickered.

"I am. Honestly, I never stopped loving you."

"I love you, Nyree Chandler," Malachi said as he leaned in to kiss her.

"We've got stuff to do," Nyree told him as she pulled away. "I got to get in the shower so we can make some runs."

"You play too much, Girl. I can't get a little tongue action."

Sticking out her tongue, she teased, "Let's take baby steps."

"Nah, I prefer to jump all in. This ain't our first time at the rodeo."

"Boy, bye." She ran out the room and upstairs into her room. As she looked through her closet, she mumbled, "I need to go shopping. I don't see anything in here I want to wear." Pushing one hanger with clothing on it, after another. Some still had tags on them, she came across a brand new pair of jeans and settled on them. Her #CrazyFaith shirt was staring her in the face. She had been meaning to order more for the ladies at church. *I can't remember everything.* Pulling the shirt off the hanger and placing it on the bed next to the jeans, she was satisfied that she had made a good choice. Picking her phone up off the nightstand she texted her assistant, Jeanine, "*Good morning, Jeanine. Please order me eight shirts in size large from Jahzara's site. Here is the link it will take you there directly:*
http://chaoticblissfragrance.blogspot.com/2015/08/you-have-to-believe-it-before-you-see.html . You can have them shipped to the spa. Thanks. Enjoy your weekend.

Nyree tossed her phone on the bed and made her way into the master bathroom and hopped into the shower. She felt so great and relaxed for the first time in months. The water was hot, and she was enjoying the beads beating down on her back. As she concluded her shower, she thought the Chaotic Bliss Body Scrub, "Better Than Sex" was a great way to exfoliate and moisturize her skin.

"Nyree. Dang, Girl, could you hurry up!" Malachi shouted as he walked into her bedroom. He quickly realized that she hadn't heard him. She was in the bathroom with the shower running. Her phone rang, and curiosity got the best of him. He leaned over the bed and saw a picture of Ivan and Nyree embraced in a hug flash across the screen with the letters IV under the picture. It kept ringing and ringing so Malachi picked up the phone and swiped the icon to reject the call. No sooner than he put the phone back where he found it did the phone begin ringing again.

"Relentless, damn," Malachi commented as he looked at the phone screen. This time, there was a picture of the spa and the words Chaotic Bliss flashed across the screen. "Hello," Malachi answered.

"Um, is this Malachi?" Jeanine asked and continued without waiting for a response, "I was trying to reach Nyree."

"She can't come to the phone right now, this is Malachi. Jeanine, what's going on?

"Um, I just got here. I'm sorry to be opening the spa late today, but I'm glad that I am. Someone broke in and trashed the supply room and your office and her office too."

"What? Are you serious? Was the alarm system engaged?"

"Yes, of course. It was armed. That's the weird thing. I deactivated it and still found this mess."

"Call the police and just wait in your vehicle. We're on our way. Don't let anyone inside. We'll be closed today. Bye."

Pounding on the bathroom door, Malachi hurried Nyree.

"What's wrong?" she asked.

"Get dressed and be downstairs in five minutes. We got to go. I will tell you about it as you drive."

"Malachi?"

"Nyree, please for once can you just do as I say and not ask one million and one questions, please," he said firmly.

Nyree dried off, moisturized her skin and wiggled into her clothes. *What shoes to wear? Oh, dang, I will just put on these since they're right here. Nikes are always a good choice. I got a feeling I'm not going to want heels on.* Nyree wore cute shoes, but heels were not a fan of hers. After breaking both of her ankles in two separate incidents, she didn't enjoy the strain heels put on her legs and feet. For a moment she remembered how she had worn heels when she was in high school daily and how she had worn heels on the campus of Indiana University Bloomington. She laughed as she recalled how she ran to the bus stop in the heels while on campus.

Nyree bounded down the stairs with her black designer bag on her shoulder. Malachi looked at her in awe. "What?" she asked.

"Nothing. I know I said five minutes, but you're not going to comb your hair?"

"Oh my gosh, I was in such a hurry." She eased over to the huge mirror in the hallway, reached into her bag pulled out a brush and a small container with hair styling gel. She dipped the brush into the container, placed the lid back on it and began brushing her hair furiously.

"Girl, it's a wonder you still got hair the way you're fighting with it," he teased.

"I'm warning you. Don't say another word. It's time for me to get my hair done. I've got to call Kelly next week. Good grief," she rambled as she brushed the hair at the nape of her neck up into a ponytail and put the hair tie around it to form a bun. Brushing the hair at her temples, she turned and looked at Malachi, "So, are my edges on fleek?"

As she dropped her hair tools back into her bag, he told her, "The stuff that comes out your mouth never ceases to surprise me. Come on we got to go for real. You got all the paperwork we talked about in your bag?"

"Yeah, what's so urgent," she asked as she armed the alarm and they walked to her truck.

"You know what if you don't mind. Let's go in my truck."

"Okay," she smirked as she pulled the keys to his vehicle out and they got in his truck.

"Not to be funny," he told her as he put on his seatbelt, "my truck got more bang than yours. And I think we need to mix up our routine and how we do things. I'm going to need you to get us to the spa safely and quickly. Hear me well, I don't want you to drive like a bat out of hell, but while you were in the shower, Jeanine called your phone, and I answered it."

"Oh okay, cool, she works for both of us."

"Yeah, and while I'm being honest, I should tell you that Ivan called too, and I rejected his call on your phone."

"Malachi, you're doing way too much. I don't know where you get off…"

"Um, back to Jeanine. She said somebody broke into the spa, trashed the supply room and our offices, so that is the urgency. And as far as Ivan goes, he can walk off into traffic on Broadway. I don't care about that dude, his feelings, nothing. So miss me with that."

Nyree turned up the radio and pushed full speed ahead to the spa. She didn't want to argue with Malachi. It seemed like every time she turned around there was more drama in her life. As soon as they pulled into the parking lot, the Gary Police Department pulled up behind them. Jeanine quickly hopped out of her black Mercedes to approach Nyree and Malachi.

"It is so good to see you, Malachi. You look great," she told him.

"Thank you, Jeanine. I feel great. Nyree and the medical team have been awesome. I thank God for them every day when I wake up and go to sleep."

Nyree's eyes bulged at Malachi's words. She never knew what was going to come out of his mouth. To hear him praising God was different. The police officers walked over to them and asked what was going on. Jeanine began telling the officers what she told Malachi.

"Open the door, please and let us go in and then we will talk," The officer who had introduced himself as Officer Brown told them. His partner, Officer Williams just stood there silently. His body language suggested that he didn't want to be on the call.

"Nyree, did you say that the system was updated a couple of weeks ago? The alarm system," Malachi said.

"Yeah, it was. Jeanine, remember when they called and told us about all the special they had and we could upgrade and get the cameras and all that."

"Yes, funny thing is, now that I remember it. The monitors that they promised; they never delivered them. When the guy came out, he said that the promotion had been such a hit that they had run out of equipment and had to back order the additional sensors we wanted. He said it was quite embarrassing, but he would call. We got the camera at the register area, but we were supposed to get some for outside and the back door area, but again they were out of equipment," Jeanine recalled, and the look on her face suggested that as she said what happened it didn't make sense.

"Okay," Malachi shook his head in disbelief, "I'm going to get to the bottom of this."

"All secure," Officer Brown hollered out to them, "why don't you all come on inside so we can complete a report and get some information."

After Jeanine finished telling the officers everything she knew and showed them the room where the camera footage could be viewed, Nyree thanked her for time and suggested she take the day off.

Malachi saw Jeanine to the door and watched her pull off. He settled back into his chair in the lobby and began telling the officers he believed that Ivan Marrick was the culprit behind all of his travesties

Officer Williams spoke up, "Mr. Chandler, you can't just go around making accusations about people because you got a feeling."

"Oh, Officer Williams this is more than a feeling, look at these texts and what about what Nyree said about the credit card statements and…"

"Mr. Chandler, look, people get into arguments all the time, love spats. How do we know this is not just a spat? Here is what you're going to have to do if you want this to stand up in a court of law. I can see you're disappointed, but you have to follow protocol."

Malachi slumped down in his chair as if he were not trying to hear. Nyree nudged him gently to encourage him to listen.

"Go ahead Officer Williams, we're listening."

Nyree had out a pen and pad and scribbled down Officer Williams' instructions. She sighed because both she and Malachi now had to file fraud claims, then they had to wait for paperwork from the financial institutions, close accounts, take the paperwork to the police department and wait and see. Nyree thanked the officers and saw them out.

"Okay, you know this is bull crap don't you?" Malachi asked.

"What I know is you having a meltdown is not going to help. Let's get this place together and see what's missing so we can file a claim with the insurance. In a minute they're going to consider us high risk and cancel us."

"Nyree, I'm tired. I really am. Look, I will be in my office."

"Fine," she told him as she began tidying up and making phone calls, retrieving faxes and looking at the camera footage.

"Malachi! Come here," she yelled.

"What's up?"

"This dude right here. I've seen him before. He was our limo driver."

"So…"

"So, I'm saying he is the connection to Ivan. Maybe Ivan put him up to this."

"Nyree, are you sure?"

"I don't forget a face."

"What's his name?"

"I don't know. He introduced himself, but I don't recall his name."

"And we still don't know why he gave him three thousand dollars in cash and why he stashed the money in your bag?"

"No. I've never seen anyone in 2016 our age pay for everything in cash. Three grand is a ridiculous amount of money to pay someone to drive you to the airport."

"But it's not a crazy amount to pay someone to kidnap somebody or commit white collar crimes," Malachi said rubbing his eyes. At times he experienced blurred vision but just rubbed his eyes to try to refocus his sight.

The sun was going down as they re-entered the house. Nyree looked at her phone and sighed, "It's Ivan again. I am so tired Malachi. I'm glad to finally be home. I'm hungry, but I don't feel like cooking. What do you think about Flamingos pizza? There's a bottle of White Sangria from Cooper's Hawk in the refrigerator. I am going to take a bath and relax. I'm sorry, I'm just tired. They will deliver the pizza if you call."

"Do you want me to come keep you company?" Malachi smiled.

"That's sweet. I just need a moment to get myself together. How are you feeling? Do you need me to get you anything? You've been running nonstop lately, and I've dumped a plethora of my emotional garbage on you, I'm sorry. I just want you to recover speedily, but successfully."

"I'm not fragile, Babe. I'm that dude you've been looking for your whole life. I'm not going to keep telling you, I'm here to show you."

Nyree walked upstairs slowly and into her walk in closet. *I know I'm out of it. I didn't take my shoes off at the door.* Shaking her head in disbelief at herself, she placed the shoes into their rightful box. When Nyree made it into the bathroom, she shut the door and let out a sigh. "God, I'm just tired. I am ready to wake up from this nightmare. Please forgive me for getting involved with Ivan. Lord, help me. I just can't do it no more," she cried as she stepped into her bubble bath.

MALACHI CHANDLER

"Okay, look I don't have a lot of time. I want you to run a more aggressive check on this bastard. I want to know where he lays at night. I want to know where his momma and them rest at night. Nyree said that his momma is in the hospital at St. Mary's in Hobart. I want to know what room she is in. Somebody needs to go out there and pay her a visit. Let her know that if her son keeps messing with me and mine it might be a double funeral since it's any day that she might check out. Are you any closer on finding out who crossed me? You know what, the pic of the guy you got going in my house… he looks like the guy we got on camera at the spa.

"Yes, I think this is the same bastard. You know I ain't never believed in coincidence. That's Nyree who thinks shit happens in isolation. Now, all this shit is connected, and you're going to help me prove it. What you say? You say the broad at the currency exchange that's been cashing those checks been going out with Ivan. Wait, wait, slow down. You got footage from the currency exchange of him coming in there to cash the checks, and she always cashes them and on top of that, they're going out. Wow." Malachi was still trying to process all the information Amber had given him. Usually, she insisted that they sit down in person for her to present the information, but she made an exception for Malachi.

"So now what?" Amber asked.

" An eye for an eye and a tooth for a tooth," Malachi responded.

"You've got to play it cool. Never let them see you coming. Lay low. Act like you're not phased and then in his weakest, most vulnerable moment, hit him and make sure he doesn't recover."

Malachi was listening, and Amber made sense. He knew just what to do. "Yep, you're right. I'm going to do just that."

"If you need any help. Just let me know what you need me and my team to do and we're there."

"Good looking. I'm going to get off of here I think that's the delivery person at the door. Later," he told Amber as he concluded the call.

"Malachi, did the pizza come?" Nyree asked as she saw him reclined on the leather sectional scrolling through his phone.

"Yep, it's in the kitchen. I made a tossed salad. Just been waiting for you to come down so we could eat."

"I thought I heard you down here talking to someone. Did the kids call?"

I don't want to lie. I really don't, but I can't tell her too much. I need her to interact with Ivan like she doesn't know shit. Every time I desire to do good, the devil comes and throws a monkey wrench in the game. "I was just on the phone dialoguing with an old friend. Trying to make sense out of life. That's all. The kids will be home around eleven or so."

"Yeah, yeah, I know that, so you don't have any more up to date information," Nyree probed.

"Nope. They're fine, but if you don't believe me call them."

"Let's eat and then I will call them."

They ate in silence. Nyree was deep in her thoughts and Malachi was trying to contemplate how he could stay one step ahead of Ivan. Why had Ivan targeted them? Something was sick and twisted about Ivan and Malachi wanted to figure it out, but he feared he didn't have time.

"You talk to dude today?"

"No," Nyree replied.

"Good. Tomorrow you talk to him. You know it's going to be hard on him. It will be Mother's Day, his mom is sick, so you're going to have to be sympathetic. By the way, where did you say he lives."

"He was staying in Crown Point, but he sold the house, and now he's downsized to a condo as he waits for his house to be completed. But you know what, it's weird because he was pressuring me into moving out of here and me and him building a house together."

"Why sell a house without having another house to go to. So, he's got a condo now. Just doesn't make sense. Nyree, did you ever see the house he sold?"

"No, never been to his house."

"And the new house, where is it going to be?"

"I don't know he always avoided the question when it comes up in conversation."

"Um, I see," he told her.

"You think I'm stupid, don't you. You just don't understand he was the perfect guy, said all the right things, did all the right things, very attentive and…"

"I don't think you're stupid. You're always so cautious. I'm just trying to figure out how you let this guy into your life so quickly and how he thought he was just going to come in and y'all would ride off into the sunset."

"Malachi, I don't know. I don't know anything anymore. I'm not sure about anything, and I don't like questioning and second guessing myself, but he would say stuff like 'You're not as smart as you think you are. Everyone pays in life, even the privileged.' He is always trying to flaunt his money. He gave India a diamond teardrop pendant. Beautiful. I had it appraised. It's coming in at a couple of thousand dollars, but these earrings he gave me…two karats of bullshit. The appraiser said they were a good pair of cubic zirconia. She said if she were not a professional she would have thought they were real. Just doesn't make sense," she told him.

Shaking his head in disbelief, stood up and pushed his chair in. "I'm tired. I'm going to lie down. Wake me up if I'm asleep when India and Christian get here."

"What?" Nyree yelled as Malachi retreated to his room.

"Don't! Just don't. You really don't want me to answer your question. Just let me continue to walk out of here."

"Walk on. That's all you do is not communicate and shut down when things get difficult. I swear the same stuff you been doing for the last twenty years," she said angrily.

"Okay, this is what you want a full blown argument. Nyree, you don't want to do this. Maybe you feeling some kinda way about ole boy, but I guaran-damn-tee you, you don't want to know what I'm thinking or feeling right now."

"Try me."

"Nyree we're talking about what you know about this man which is apparently nothing. You bring him to your house but never been to his house. You go out of town with him. I'm fighting for my life, and you say you will come back in town when you get done having fun. I'm talking to you about how suspect he is and you have the audacity to tell me about some fake jewelry he gives you, but an expensive piece of jewelry he gives to India. You've been knowing this cat for five minutes and have him around our children. I don't know if he's a pedophile or what. You got this clown of suspicious character around your teenage daughter. Yeah, I'm now questioning you and your character. I mean I thought you were better than that. I get it, we all have needs that need to be fulfilled, but at what cost, Nyree? What cost?"

Nyree walked over to Malachi and slapped his so hard that he foamed at the mouth. "You really got a lot of damn nerve to question my integrity. When your ass couldn't do for yourself, you forget who was there for you?" Shoving him forcefully in his chest, her head came to the middle of his chest, and she looked up at him, and her eyes dared him to respond.

Familiar with that look, he instructed her, "Get out my face Nyree. Walk your tail on up those steps. Go now. I don't want to do or say something I am going to regret. Nyree, go and go now," he backed up a couple of feet to allow her plenty of distance to pass him. He stood fixed in that spot and watched her go upstairs. His eyes burned, and his hands trembled as his eyes zeroed in on the Annie Lee "Love Song" painting on the wall in the living room. When they woke up in bed together this morning he had no idea the day would end like this.

IVAN MARRICK

Ivan walked down the hallway of the hospital toward his mother's room. It was seven-thirty, and he had just arrived. His goal was to have made it here earlier, but one thing happened after another today. India had called him earlier in the day on her way to Six Flags and thanked him for renting the party bus for her and her friends. She was ever so grateful. It was her senior year, and she wanted to do something over the top.

No sooner than he hung up with India, did he get the dreaded, anticipated call from Colin. Colin's parole hearing on April 29th hadn't gone in Colin's favor. Colin was very articulate and got to the point fast, "I helped you and you were supposed to help me. Nyree didn't speak up for me at my parole hearing like you promised. You didn't keep your end of the deal. So, I think something needs to be done about that. Wouldn't you agree?"

Ivan looked at his Edge7, nodded his head at the screen and ended the call from Colin. *I know what I got to do. Got to get real low. I got to get back under the radar.*

Walking past the nurse's station one of the nurses called out, "Hi Ivan. We didn't think you were coming today. Usually, you're here by now."

"Yeah, I know. Business crisis had me tied up. Who's her nurse?"

"Tammy, she's doing rounds right now. When she comes back around I will have her come in and update you."

"Okay," he said and walked down to the last room on the left. The room was filled with nine vases. Each containing long stemmed black roses. There was a card in one of the vases. It read *Tomorrow ain't promised.*

Ivan looked around as if someone were watching him. He walked into the bathroom to make sure no one was hiding. As ridiculous as it was, he thought someone was hiding under his mother's bed. He got down on his hands and knees to have a thorough look under the bed. As he got up off the floor, he dusted off the knees of his khaki pants and adjusted his polo shirt.

"Ivan, is everything okay?" Tammy asked as she looked at him puzzled.

Startled to see Tammy, "Um, yeah, yeah. I dropped something, but it's all good."

"Let me see if I can help you find it."

"No, I don't want to worry you with that. I'm sure it will turn up. These flowers, what do you know about them?"

"Black roses signify death, mourning, revenge…pure evil. I guess you could find some beauty in them. Nine vases of them. Spiritually nine means finality or completeness. I think the sender was trying to send a morbid message that death is coming and soon. There is a total of 108 roses in this room. Did you know that the diameter sun, when multiplied by the number 108, equals the distance between the Sun and Earth? Now watch this when you multiply the diameter of the moon by the number 108 that equals the distance between the Earth and the Moon. So again the sender is sending the message that your world as you know it is about to be shaken up."

"Damn Tammy, I just wanted to know if you knew where these flowers came from. Who sent them?"

"Don't know. No one knows. They were delivered by a local florist, but no information was provided when our staff asked. I was not here, but during turn over no one knew anything. I'm told your dad came by today and caused a real nasty scene when he was told he couldn't visit."

"Oh really. You all know he's not authorized to see my mom."

"He was informed of that, but he insisted he had every right to be here and asked if he could provide the secret password could he stay. Since he knew the password we assumed you must have changed your mind about him. Additionally, we called you several times today but only received your voice mail. Your mother has been unresponsive."

"You think because she is not able to move or talk she does not know what's going on?"

"Ivan, we've had this conversation several times, so I won't get into it with you tonight. Are you staying tonight?"

"Yes," Ivan said not wanting to hear her opinions.

"I will bring you some blankets. Have you eaten today? Can I get you something?"

"Can I get a sandwich or something?"

"Sure. I will be back shortly."

Ivan reached into his pocket and pulled out a medicine bottle. Opening the cap, he watched the yellow pills fall into the palm of his hand. He swallowed two pills as if they were candy. They went down so quickly and easily that water was not necessary. Sitting in the recliner, he reached over and grabbed his mother's hand and recited the lyrics to Tupac's song, "Dear Mama."

Thirty minutes later, Tammy returned with chicken salad on a bagel, a sprite, and three blankets.

"Good looking, Tammy. I'm going to start a foundation in my mother's name. I want you to be the President. You have been so good to my mother. I will pay you generously," Ivan smiled. *Where did that lie come from, Ivan found himself thinking.*

The young woman who looked liked she could have graduated nursing school yesterday tossed her blond hair and said, "Oh my gosh, Ivan, I'm flattered. Oh, what an honor."

Sure, would be one if it were true. "Yes and I talked with a Senator down state and we're trying to get a hospital wing named after my mom here in Northwest Indiana."

"Oh my," Tammy perked up. Then the unit phone called her, and she excused herself and walked out the room to take the call.

Ivan waved her off and told her thanks. "We will talk soon," he called after her. Ivan devoured the sandwich in three bites. Famished probably didn't accurately describe his level of hunger. He sent Nyree another text. *I need her. Why is she ignoring me? What do I have to do to get her attention?*

Ivan threw his trash into the trash can. Then he reached under the mound of trash and tossed the Edge7 phone in the bottom of the trash as well.

NYREE CHANDLER

The pounding on her door awakened her out of her sleep. She had stayed up into the wee hours of the morning with India and Christian talking about the weekend. All she desired on this beautiful morning was a few more hours of sleep. The pounding continued. She missed the days of having a housekeeper in the house, she would not have allowed all this noise.

"Yes," she mumbled from under the mound of covers over her head. It was seventy-degree weather, but she still required the blankets over her at night. She found it comforting.

"Good morning," Malachi sang.

"Umph," she mumbled.

He pounced on the bed and lifted the mound of blankets from over her. "When I say good morning you say it back to me, not umph," he told her.

"Malachi, I'm tired. Good morning, now I'm going back to sleep and give me my covers back. It's cold."

He laughed. She always swore it was cold when he took her out of her cocoon.

"Happy Mother's Day. And I want to apologize for last night. I was frustrated. I said some hurtful things, and I should not have."

"No, you said what you felt, and I'm sorry. I apologize for what I said," she told him.

"Come on and get up so we can go to church. Everybody's waiting on you."

Nyree rubbed her eyes as she realized Malachi was as the old folks say, "Cleaner than the board of health" in his three-piece suit. Freshly shaven too. She smirked, "Umph."

"You're going to church? Oh my, what's really going on?"

"Nyree, stop playing. I believe in God. I just don't always act like I'm His child, but I know he spared my life for a reason. I've been given a second chance at life, and I'm not going to fuc…mess it up. Don't look at me like that. I've still got to be delivered from some thangs, but I believe in God, and I know there is a God."

"Okay, just a few more minutes of sleep. God answers prayers. I've been praying for this moment for a lifetime," she told him as she rolled back into her cocoon.

He snatched the covers again, "Come on, Nyree, for real. I want us to go to church as a family."

This would have been great fifteen years ago, but I guess better late than never. Oh here goes all the social media notifications and text notifications. Yes, it is Mother's Day. I feel blessed, but this phone is going to drive me crazy.

"I picked your outfit out down to the shoes. Don't look at me like that. You know I got good taste. Come on Bae, all you got to do is get showered. Everything else is taken care of. I even made your coffee like you like it."

"You made my coffee."

"Well actually no, it's a little instant thingy I found in the cabinet, but yeah, I got your coffee ready."

Nyree slid from under the cover and dragged to the bathroom.

When she stepped out the shower, her bed was made up and true to his word, Malachi had chosen the perfect outfit with matching shoes. He had put together a nice ensemble. After dressing and styling her hair as best, she could, she winked at herself in the mirror. As she strolled down the stairs, India called, "Okay, MaMa, I see you. Get it, girl, you better work that stairway."

"India, you are a mess," Nyree laughed.

"I get it from my momma. Happy Mother's Day," India hugged her mother after she finally made it down the flight of twelve stairs. Nyree hugged her back.

"Thank you Honey Child and where is Bruh Bruh?"

"Here I be, Mamaja. Here's a little something, something for you on this most glorious day," Christian told his mother as he handed her a small box. He motioned for her to follow him into the kitchen. Nyree sat at the island picked up her coffee cup and sipped.

"Malachi, you did this?"

"Yeah, I mean it's just coffee, right? Who can mess up coffee?"

Nyree cut her eyes at him. "Okay, Christian told me how much cream and sugar to do."

Nyree tore open the box. "The wrapping paper was nice," she said as she opened the box. "Oh, my. You guys. Oh my, this is the replica of the butterfly ring my daddy gave my momma. I helped him pick it out over forty years ago."

"Yes, we thought you deserved to have your own butterfly ring because that's who and what you are. You take bad situations and cause them to blossom into something beautiful. You have the butterfly effect on people's lives," Christian told her, he continued, "I'm a living witness, and I love you, Ma" he hugged her.

She sniffled. "I love you so much. I love you too, India, come over her and give me a hug. You know what, y'all gonna mess up my makeup and I'm not going to be able to go to church."

Malachi dabbed her face with some tissue, "The devil is a lie. Cry again if you want to and you'll just be up in there looking like you were in the club all night. They will be calling you down to the prayer line early."

Nyree smacked Malachi on the arm and said, "You are too silly. You feel like driving?"

"Yeah, I think I'm up to it. I got a surprise for you after church."

"You know what, I don't know how much more I can take."

Nyree left church feeling exhilarated. She had about four pages of notes in her mini notebook that she carried to church. The best part of the service had been when Malachi went down to the altar and gave his life to the Lord. Nyree had wanted this so badly for Malachi, but she just never thought the day would come when he would surrender his life to the Lord. As she sat in the front seat of the truck, she looked in the mirror and tried to fix her face. All the crying she had done when Malachi was at the altar had left her eyes red, and mascara streaks up and down her face.

"I don't know where we're going, but I hope it involves food," Nyree told Malachi as they drove down U.S. 30. He didn't respond.

When the truck pulled into the parking lot of House of Kobe, she smiled. Then she noticed that there were not any cars in the lot. "They're not opened, Malachi. There's not one car in this lot."

"I am going to let you out right here, go up to the door and see if someone is in there."

"It's dark as ever. NO one is in there."

"Nyree, could you just check while I park. Christian and India go with your mom."

"Tck, I don't see why you want to have us looking crazy Malachi, but we will humor you."

"Thank you," Malachi said as he parked.

Malachi hurried to the door and saw his family standing with a waiter at the front of the restaurant. There were red roses everywhere. The waiter smiled and said, "Mr.Chandler are we ready to proceed?"

"Yes," Malachi said.

Squinting her eyes at Malachi, Nyree questioned, "What's going on here?"

"This way, ma'am," the waiter instructed as he walked to an area in the middle of the restaurant. They were the only people in the restaurant.

Sitting down, Nyree announced with a questioning tone, " I thought you all were closed?"

He laughed, "We are."

"Huh?" Nyree asked.

"But we opened just for you."

"Malachi?" Nyree asked.

"Sh…" Malachi answered.

"This man love you. He buy out the whole restaurant for the evening for you and your family," the waiter said.

"What? Malachi!"

"Just learn to relax and enjoy life. You haven't been listening to anything I said this weekend. I'm back. No worries."

Nyree was in awe. She promised herself to live in the moment and enjoy the moment. Her mind began to worry about all the drama that she and Malachi thought Ivan had incited. *Tomorrow will be here soon enough, and that's the time to deal with it. Now just enjoy the moment.*

Their chef stood by the hibachi grill making preparations to cook. Nyree could see that he was serious about his job, but he performed each task with pride and grace. He loved his job, and it was evident. Nyree was sipping on a pina colada, and it was quite tasty. Malachi and the children were chattering away, and all just seemed to be well in the world. Chef did the little trick with the fire appearing to be a volcano off the meat and vegetable mixture on the grill. Now he was ready to perform tricks. He told Christian to open his mouth, and he tossed a shrimp. It fell into his mouth. "Your turn the chef told Malachi." With a shake of the head, Malachi declined to participate. "Aw, Dad you're no fun," India whined hoping that he would reconsider.

Malachi chuckled, "Well worse has been said of me so I'm no fun today."

The chef continued to move on and suggested India have a try. The shrimp missed her mouth. She bubbled over with laughter. "Now, for the lady of the hour," the chef directed his shrimp throwing skills toward Nyree's mouth.

"Oh yeah," she squealed when it made it into her mouth. Then she did the Cabbage Patch dance which no one at the seating area was prepared for. She smiled. Nyree was on cloud nine. Life was grand. She felt so special that Malachi would orchestrate this for her.

Turning to Malachi, she told him, "This is the first time, I ever was able to catch a shrimp. Thank you so much for putting this dinner together. I really appreciate everything."

He hugged her. He was more affectionate here lately than she ever remembered. "Well, I'm glad you could experience that first time with me. You know you're my first love." His confession took Nyree aback. It just seemed so random and came from out of nowhere.

"This has been the best Mother's Day," Nyree told Malachi as she kicked her heels off at the front door. They had just left from visiting her mother along with their children. For the first time in forever, she and her mother hadn't exchanged hurtful words.

"Where are you going?" Malachi asked as he noticed her ascending up the staircase with heels in hand.

"I'm going to go upstairs and get out of these clothes. You know I don't like having pantyhose on for too long." She pouted.

Malachi chuckled at her comment. "Well don't be all day. I got Maggie Moo in the freezer."

Nyree spun around so quickly on the stair's that she nearly lost her balance. "Don't play with me! How did you come across Maggie Moo?"

Malachi rubbed his hands together as if he were trying to generate heat from the friction. "Haha, you want to know, do you?" His voice sounded like something out of a vampire movie. "All I can say is if you like Maggie Moo like you say you do, you will be back in the kitchen in a New York minute."

Nyree yelled over the banister, once she reached the top of the staircase, "What's a New York minute?"

"You're going to show me what a New York minute is by making it back down here before I can blink an eye."

"Now you know…"

"Yes, I know you can be slower than molasses, but tonight you're going to turn over a new leaf."

Nyree walked into her bedroom and put on a purple Nike warm up suit. This was one of the outfits Ivan liked seeing her wear. She sat on the edge of the bed as she put on her sock and thought about Ivan. She hadn't had an opportunity to respond to any of the texts he had sent today. Nyree slipped on her Nike shoes and then began tying them when the phone rang. No need to look at the screen it was Ivan calling. He was the only person who had the Beyonce's "Sorry" ringtone on her phone.

Tapping the blue tooth to accept the call, she spoke hurriedly, "Hey Ivan, how are you?"

There was silence on the other end. "Hello! Hello!" Nyree yelled. She was certain that he was still on the phone as the Bluetooth hadn't informed her that the call had ended.

"Nyree, can you come to the hospital. Mother is no longer with us."

"Huh?" Nyree was stunned.

"My mother took her last breath about five minutes ago. I got to call the nurses and tell them. Please, I know I have no right to ask you this, but please can you come to the hospital. I don't have anyone else I can call."

"I'm so sorry, Ivan. I'm so sorry."

"Thank you, but can you please come?" Ivan pressed.

Tears flowed down Nyree's face. She couldn't imagine the pain, hurt, sorrow and other emotions that Ivan was experiencing. "Yes, I will be there."

"Thank you, Sweetie," he said slowly.

Nyree didn't recall walking down the stairs and past Malachi's room. When she got to the door, he was on her heels. "I see you with your purse, where are you going? What about Maggie Moo?"

"Um, sorry, some other time maybe."

"What's wrong?"

"Ivan's situation changed. I got to go to the hospital," she said speaking in code just in case the children were listening.

"Oh, I see," Malachi said exaggeratedly, "are you going to be okay to drive? Do you need a driver?"

"No, I'm fine," Nyree lied. She began to wonder what if she and Malachi were wrong for thinking Ivan was behind all their tragedy. What if Ivan was just a man coping with watching his mother die and now dealing with her death?

"When you're on your way home, call me," Malachi instructed Nyree as she eased out the front door.

"I will," she told him.

IVAN MARRICK

"Yeah, what's up, Sweetie? You here?" Ivan asked Nyree.

"Yes, I am about to get in the elevator. I'm calling you like you asked me to do when I got here," Nyree told him.

"Yes, yes, I'm down the hall in the waiting room, just come down there. You know where it is right?"

"Yes, the same one we sat in the other day, right?" Nyree questioned.

"Yes. I'm in here. I heard the elevator ding. I'm going to see you in a few," Ivan told Nyree and then hung up his flip phone.

Ivan was pacing back and forth when Nyree entered the waiting room. "Ivan, I'm so sorry," she told him as she approached him. He looked at her in amazement. "Thank you, Sweetie, for coming. I hope I haven't ruined your Mother's Day. By the way Happy Mother's Day. I texted you earlier but…"

"Thank you. Let's sit down. How are you?"

"I don't know. Luis from the facility is in the room with my mom. I don't think you've ever met him. Come on let's go down there so you can meet him. Plus I want you to see mom. I tried to fix her hair earlier, you've got to see what I did. I told you my grandmomma was a beautician right? Yeah, she would be proud of how I fixed mom up," Ivan rambled as he grabbed Nyree's hand and started walking out of the room.

Nyree paused, "You know what, maybe I should just stay here and let you handle what you need to do. I don't want to be in the way."

"You won't be in the way. What, you don't want to be here? You're just like every woman whom I cared about in my life. They all get mad and leave me. First granny, mom, and now you. You remind me of my mom. There's this softness about you, but such strength. My mom had a beautiful set of pearls. You should have them."

"It's not that I don't want to be here. I'm here right? I'm surprised you want me here after you sent me all those mean text messages. I'm an opportunist, all I do is take. You were going to ruin my name and my company, remember?" Nyree reminded him, and each word she spoke got louder and louder.

Ivan sighed, "Damn, you know I wasn't for real. You know I would never do anything to hurt you. Come on and walk with me," he convinced her as he clasped her hand and lead her down the hallway.

As they walked into the room, Luis was writing something in a notebook. He began shutting it when Ivan started the introductions. "It's good to meet you," Luis told Nyree, "I've heard a lot about you from Ivan."

Nyree extended her hand and shook Luis's hand. "Thank you. I hope it was all good," she smiled nervously.

"Of course it was, sweetheart," Ivan told her. Turning his attention to Luis, Ivan asked, "Do I need to sign anything?"

"No, no, everything is good. I guess I'm going to head home now that Nyree is here. If you need anything, or we can be of assistance don't hesitate to call us. I'm sorry that Ms.Charity is… you know she's not hurting now. She's at rest," Luis said as he turned and looked at Charity. Luis was only thirty-six years old, but he looked old and tired. Ivan couldn't help but think that the fact that Luis had a wife and four small children probably added to the stress and worn look.

"Thanks, Luis. Yes, go home and try to enjoy the rest of Mother's Day with your wife and family. I will never celebrate Mother's Day again. I will be haunted by this day," He said truthfully as Luis quietly exited the room.

Nyree sat in a chair quietly as she took in the whole scene. Her feet seemed to shake nervously. Ivan was glad she was here. He grabbed his mother's hand, and tears filled his eyes. "You were my rock. I don't know what I'm going to do without you," he said and then laid his head on her chest. Nyree put her head down and wiped her eyes. She excused herself and went into the restroom.

When Nyree came out of the bathroom, Ivan was sitting in the reclining chair.

"You okay, Sweetie. I'm waiting on a call from the funeral home. I'm so glad I paid for her funeral in advance. I don't think I could do this now."

"Hi, we're from Guy and Allen Funeral Home," two African-American gentlemen dressed in black announced as they came into the room with a stretcher and black bag. The taller man started adjusting the rails on the hospital bed. As they began to move Charity's body, Ivan began to assist.

"We have it, you don't have to..." the taller man spoke as he bumped Charity's head in the midst of transporting her to the stretcher.

"Watch what you're doing? You just bumped my momma's head. Come on now," Ivan was furious.

Nyree walked over to Ivan and suggested that maybe they leave during this process.

"No, no, I'm not going to leave my momma. She's going to leave me, but I'm not going to leave her."

In what seemed like seconds, the funeral home associates had Charity strapped to the stretcher with the black blanket over her. Ivan sighed as he noticed they didn't put her in the body bag. Maybe they will do it when they get to the transport vehicle.

"Excuse me, I got to go to the bathroom," he told Nyree. Soon as he made it into the bathroom, he leaned over the commode and let everything inside of him hit the water in the toilet bowl. When he was satisfied that there was nothing left to bless the toilet with, Ivan flushed the toilet twice. He made his way to the sink and washed his hands, his face and rinsed his mouth. Looking into the mirror, he noticed his eyes were bloodshot. *I'm still fine as hell, but I look like I've been in a fight and got my ass beat. I always get the last lick. Always. I've got to go out here and face Nyree. I wonder if she knows what I've done. Nah, she couldn't. If she did, there is no way she would be here. Tomorrow I've got to see what's up with the life insurance policy and the will. No, I will wait until after the funeral. No, I need to know. I've got to see about my inheritance.*

"Let's go. Can you drop me off at the crib? I let my boy hold my car, so I don't have any way home," Ivan lied.

****

In his mind, he recalled why his boy was really holding his car. Ivan had failed to supply Onyx for the odd jobs he had performed. Onyx had taken care of Rayna and Malachi as instructed. Ivan had paid him three thousand dollars, but Onyx required twenty thousand dollars for Operation Rayna and fifteen thousand dollars for Operation Chandler which included Malachi and Nyree. "I gave you the Friends and Family discount, Ivan. Now you're playing me. No, no. I still have to pay Randall for his assistance. Three thousand dollars is all you have given me to this date and not to mention the other operations I assisted you in. You owe at least two hundred thousand dollars, and that may be lowballing it," Onyx had told him two weeks ago.

"Onyx, I told you I got you and as soon as the funeral occurs and the will is read you will be set. The construction company is being restructured, and you know the money is going to come in soon as it's up and running again," Ivan spoke.

"Look, you may have the gift of gab with people, but you're not going to run that flim-flam bullshit on me. Everybody knows that you don't even own the company. You sold your shares of the company, so what are you talking about?"

Ivan recalled feeling stunned that Onyx had called him out like that. Usually, Onyx went along with whatever Ivan said truth or lie. *Onyx has grown some balls.*

"So this is what you're going to do. That Mercedes you got, you're going to sign it over to me. We're going to the Department of Motor Vehicles right now. This is just the beginning of the takeover, Ivan. You think you can go through life without paying. Wrong answer."

****

Ivan felt nervous as he and Nyree walked on the sidewalk of the hospital toward where she had parked. He stopped and grabbed her hand. "Look, I just want to thank you for being here. I know I can be an asshole, but I love you," he told her. He was shocked that he had allowed the words to come out. The look on her face suggested that either she was shocked to hear the word coming out of his mouth.

"I said it, and I meant it. A man pretty much knows the first time he encounters a woman how he feels. He knows what he wants from her before he even opens his mouth to speak. When I had a second chance with you I knew I had to jump on it," Ivan told her. It was true in more than one way. He had to make a romantic move as well as a financial move. He hugged her and tried to kiss her. Nyree pulled back out of the embrace. "Come on, let's get to the truck. I have to get home to the children and make sure they're ready for tomorrow."

"Oh," Ivan raised an eyebrow. Nyree had never been so abrupt with him before. "Did I do something to offend you?"

"Ivan, you know what, honestly you have offended me on several occasions and why we need to discuss it right now just doesn't seem appropriate."

Ivan didn't know what to say as he settled into the passenger's seat which was pulled back significantly. A tinge of jealousy fell upon him as he imagined that he was sitting where Malachi had so often sat.

"So where am I driving to?" Nyree asked as she pulled out of the parking lot and began driving toward Merrillville.

"Yeah, my mom had this little spot in Merrillville. I just kept her apartment for her because I always thought she was coming home. It's nothing much because a lot of times she would stay with me, but just so she could have that sense of independence, you know?"

Nyree hunched her shoulders as she drove and reached down into her bag and pulled out her glasses. "As I get older, I find myself needing these more and more," she told Ivan.

When they approached Sixty-first Avenue and Broadway he told her, "You're going to want to get in the left turning lane. We're going to Seventy-third and Broadway."

"Hm," she remarked.

"Yeah, like I said it's just a little place that she had."

"I see and how are things progressing with your house? I would love to see the construction and what's going on with it."

"Yeah, yeah, yeah. You know with everything that's been going on I just put the project on pause. It's been so much Nyree, you can't imagine what I've been going through. Well, now mom, is at rest," he told her as she pulled into the lot.

"Right here is my building. Mom's building," he quickly self-corrected as Nyree put the truck into park.

Sensing that she was coming in Ivan spoke up, "Well, I know you were anxious to get home to the kids. Tell my angels I send my love."

"Yes, I will. I can come in and get you settled. You look like you could use a good home-cooked meal," she told him.

" I really don't have an appetite. Thanks, Sweetie. I got some phone calls to make and whew, yeah, it's been a day and see, there goes your phone ringing. Did I ruin your Mother's Day? I'm sorry," he told her. *I slipped the word sorry but it's true, I am sorry based on virtue of the definition. My motives toward Nyree are not and have not been pure. Hell, my motives toward my own mother were not even pure.*

Ivan walked into the apartment and looked at the mess he had in the living room. He had pulled out boxes which contained important papers, and they were in various locations around the room. *I've got to call mom's friends and let them know she's passed on. I've got to call family members. They all know what was going on with her, why should I call them. They should have been calling me to check on me. It's cool, when I get this money they better not call then. Dad, should I call him? Maybe I will. He should know that his wife died, shouldn't he? I mean really the way I'm feeling, he could just read it in the paper when everyone else does.*

Walking over to his small makeshift bar, Ivan poured Remy 1738 into a glass tumbler. He took a seat at his desk, pulled out the middle drawer and found the amber colored pill bottle. "Ah," he sighed as he looked into the bottle and saw four small yellow pills. Disappointment loomed over him as he was nearly out of Xanax and couldn't get a refill without seeing a doctor. He would cross that bridge when he got to it, he thought as he popped the pill in his mouth and chased it with the liquor he had poured himself seconds ago. Ivan called a few aunts and uncles. Texts were coming in from cousins. His cash stash was at one hundred thousand dollars. He was doing okay, but his worry was not about the present, it was about the future. Working a nine-to-five was not in his vocabulary. *I thought Nyree would be sympathetic to me, but she seemed so different today. She was saying all the right things, but her physical actions were distant. I wonder if she knows what I did. Huh. I did it all for her. I just wanted to have something to bring to the table. When I collect my momma's life insurance and get the money from the will, I will be able to match Nyree dollar for dollar. I bet you then I will have her attention. She will stop looking at me like I'm a piece of chewed gum on the ground. I've only been home an hour. It's ten o'clock, feels like it's much later. I just want to stop crying and go to sleep. I hope I fall asleep soon. My cocktail should be kicking in soon.*

Ivan was awakened by the "Tweet On It or Speak On It" segment on WGCI. He found himself rubbing his eyes. He thought his ears were deceiving him. The radio personalities: Kendra G., Kyle, and Leon were talking with listeners regarding the issue of this female dating this guy, and the guy she was dating was taking a bath with her nine-year-old son. Apparently, the father of the child got wind of this inappropriate behavior and was livid. *What kind of momma would allow this foolishness? Hell, I can't say nothing.*

My momma knew I was being sexually abused by her boyfriend's friends, and she did nothing. She always conveniently was never home when the abuse occurred, but she had to know. She had to have seen the way Uncle J.J. looked at me. Never did she protect me. I'm still angry and bitter about this. Wonder what they got. I think this is the real reason I don't have children. I don't want to carry on the piss poor parenting tradition that Ivan and Charity started. I need that father to be more than angry. He needs to go get his son. I hope that child doesn't endure what I endured.

Ivan shuffled into the second bedroom and lifted weights and did some sit ups. His Ralph Lauren pajama pants hung nicely off his waist. He scooted to his room to put on an undershirt so that he could make a pot of coffee. The thought of people including himself not being properly clothed while preparing food or drink in the kitchen repulsed him.

Ivan took three sips of the coffee and dumped the remaining fluid in the sink. Black coffee was good, but this was too strong. Making coffee had never been his forte. Rayna made the best coffee in the world. He was missing his partner in crime this morning. "Rayna, why did you have to ruin everything? You were my heart, girl!" *She was the only female who really loved me and cared about me. I could count on her to do whatever was necessary. I don't know why she went and messed everything up. No time for that I got to call Shauna Buchanan about this will.*

Ivan could hear the hustle and bustle of those outside. Cars were zipping in and out of the parking lot. A school bus just zoomed past. He missed his house. It had been quiet and secluded. Now he was amongst people in a busy complex.

Ivan prided himself on being private. His heart was beating rapidly. Had he messed up by letting Nyree know where he lived? Ivan's mind was all over the place. "Focus, IV, focus. Shauna Buchanan. Shauna Buchanan. Got to call Shauna Buchanan. It's only eight o'clock. I doubt she's in her office this early. Okay, game plan. Take a shower. Call Nyree. Call Shauna Buchanan and go to the funeral home."

After getting showered, Ivan felt like a weight had been lifted from him. *Okay, I got to find something to wear and go to the hospital and…no, no, I don't have to go to the hospital. Mother is not there anymore.* Tears saturated his face. He reached down by the bed and picked up the bottle of Remy 1738, he had brought it into the bedroom before taking his shower. Ivan lifted it to his lips and guzzled the liquid down as if it were Kool-Aid. Beating his chest, he screamed because the burn from the liquid was tearing his insides apart. Shaking off the pain, he brought the bottle back up to his lips and repeated the process. *I should call Onyx and tell him about Mother. Nah, fuck, Onyx. I don't fuck with him no more. In my time of need, he turned his back on me. It's a new day for Ivan Marrick. It's time for me to initiate payback on all those who did me wrong. I spared a lot of people because of my mother. Now that's she gone it's on and popping like popcorn.*

"Nyree, what's up? So are you going to come with me to the funeral home?" Ivan bombarded her with a series of questions as soon as she answered the phone. "You sure?" He asked. Ivan was picking up a vibe from Nyree that he didn't like. "I mean, I'm asking because you hesitated. I mean if you going to act all funny style, fuck it. I don't need this. My mother just died. I reach out to the only person I thought would be there for me in my time of need, but it's good. If you're too busy, then cool. Go on ahead with your perfect life. You know I've been there for you. Who do you think made that anonymous donation to your foundation for the girls? You get in trouble you see who your real friends are. Don't worry about it." Ivan hung up and prepared himself to go to the funeral home.

Ivan rocked back and forth in the chair as he sat across from Tamela Allen in her office at Guy&Allen Funeral Home. He always thought he would bury his father due to his father's lifestyle. Death is inevitable he knew it, he just never thought he would be sitting here making preparations for his mother. "Excuse me, Tamela and Mr. Marrick, I have Mrs. Chandler here she wants to join the meeting," the receptionist spoke as she peeked through the door with Nyree on her heels.

Ivan stood up, and when he caught a glimpse of Nyree he said, "Girl, get in here." Pulling the vacant seat out next to him, he motioned for her to have a seat. When Nyree took her seat, he put his arm around her and allowed his head to rest on her shoulder, he smiled, then he sat up. He kissed her cheek and said, "Girl, I love you." Turning to Tamela he told her, " I love this girl." Grabbing Nyree's hand, he redirected his attention to Tamela. "Okay, now I can think. My better half is here." Nyree reached over and grabbed Ivan's hand. "Yes, Hon, I'm here so how are things going?"

Tamela spoke, "Well, we need to know about the church. He's not sure what church."

"Ivan, what church did your mother belong to? Just have it there. Didn't you tell me your uncle was the pastor of a church here in the city."

Damn, Nyree doesn't forget shit. I forgot I told that lie. I don't have an uncle that's a pastor. We used to go to church all the time, but I doubt they even still remember us at that church. I can't remember the last time mom went to church.

"I will tell you about that later. I don't think I want it at his church," Ivan shrugged.

"Oh," Nyree said shocked.

"Well, then you have to provide information that you want to be placed in the newspaper. Also, do you want a picture included that's extra."

"Money is no object. Yes, we will have a picture included. I don't know what I want to include in the obituary. Okay, here is what I want it to say, "Charity C. Marrick, sixty-one years old of Merrillville, Indiana passed away on May 8, 2016, in Hobart, Indiana. Charity graduated from Roosevelt High School in 1973 and attended Purdue University. She was a member of one of the Divine Nine sororities. Charity worked at local financial institutions in the Gary area. She is preceded in death by parents, Michelle and Samuel Greene. She leaves to cherish her memory loving son, Ivan Marrick IV of Merrillville, Indiana; brother, Samuel Greene, of Nashville, Tennessee; sister, Charisse Turner of Atlanta, Georgia; one niece, one nephew and a host of loving family and friends. Let's do visitation on Friday from twelve noon to eight in the evening. Let's see can we have the funeral here Saturday. That will give people from out of town time to get here."

Tamela looked shocked, "Mr. Marrick, we can put all the information in the obituary, but we need it in written form. We will write it up just as you have it written. I'm looking at the schedule so far we have one funeral scheduled here on Saturday. We can get you in for Saturday, but we would need payment in full today. We also need to view the caskets."

"Ivan, I thought you said that the funeral expenses were already paid for?" Nyree questioned.

"They were, but there were some things that I wanted added on and needed to be different but yeah, it's no big deal. In fact, Tamela, go ahead and give me a total."

"Let's go to the casket room first then once you pick it out we can go from there." After they finished picking out a mint green casket lined with pink, they returned to Tamela's office. Sitting where they had sat before, Ivan sighed.

"Okay, Mr. Marrick, just let me total some things here," she said as she keyed in numbers on a form and then computed them on her adding machine from the last century. With a tight smile she pushed the form to him with a list of itemized cost and said, "Well, it will be seven thousand nine hundred fifty-six dollars."

Ivan reached into both front pockets of his khaki pants and gave one band of money for Nyree to hold and began counting another band of money. When the band of money in his hands ran out, he sighed, "Okay, that's five thousand dollars right there. Double check that." Tamela quietly counted the money, and when she got to the last hundred dollars she said, "Okay, that's five thousand."

"Yep," he nodded. "Okay, Sweetie, give me that other band." Ivan counted out the remaining balance, gave it to Tamela and was still able to return two thousand dollars to his pockets. He rested in his chair as he watched Tamela count it out. "Okay, I just need your signature here," Tamela said as she pointed to the line where she needed him to sign. Nyree's eyes were focused on the paperwork. Ivan said, "Did I do good, Sweetie? Here I'm going to give you this paperwork to hold."

Nodding and accepting the paperwork in her hand, Nyree responded, "Okay, of course. You know you don't really need to be walking around with all that money in your pocket."

"It's all good, Sweetie, nobody is going to touch me," he smiled, "I'm like Drew Peterson, I'm untouchable." The laugh that came from him was sinister and eerie. Nyree and Tamela looked at him in disbelief. It seemed that they found his comparison of himself to Drew Peterson to be reprehensible.

"Well, Mr. Marrick, I think we're done here. If you need anything, do not hesitate to contact us. Here is my card with my direct number. We need that information written up, so if you can have that to us today, that would be great. In fact, my email is on the card, just email it over to save yourself a trip. Now, I'm stressing today so we can have it to the newspapers because you want to run it Thursday and Friday."

"Yes," he nodded, "I will have it to you." They walked out of Tamela's office and down the hallway to the front door. Nyree rushed out the door and exhaled when they got outside. "Hey Sweetie, thanks so much for being here. Can you walk next door with me to pick out flowers?"

"Um, yeah, sure. I was such a mess when I had to make preparations for my father, but I had my brother there. I used to wish I were an only child. I can't imagine how you're feeling. How's your dad holding up?" Nyree questioned.

"What are you asking me about him for?" Ivan questioned as they approached the door of Allen's Florists.

It was becoming quite warm, and Nyree began fanning herself as she grabbed the door knob. "I just asked. That is your father. I noticed when you were providing the information to Tamela you didn't mention him. They were still married despite how you might feel about him."

"He broke her heart. Never did anything, but cause her sadness and despair, so why should he be mentioned?"

"Omitting him doesn't mean he doesn't exist. Is this how your mom felt or is this how you feel?" Nyree was digging deep for answers. Ivan didn't want to address her question. "Come on. I have way too much to be concerned with. He's probably somewhere shooting up or smoking a rock. I spent a lot of money trying to get him rehabilitated. I'm not going to talk about this here. What do you think about this casket arrangement?" He asked as he pointed to a display.

They spent an hour in the florist shop picking out flowers. Ivan was very indecisive. Nyree would give her opinion and then wait patiently for him to agree, disagree or make other suggestions. The florist was very helpful, and Ivan was careful to make her remember his mother.

"Yes, yes, I remember Charity. We went to school together. Uh huh, you know she still had an outstanding balance from your grandmother's funeral. Yep, three hundred dollars. We just went ahead and sent the flowers over to your grandmother's funeral because we knew Charity," Ms. Allen said looking disappointed.

Ivan felt embarrassed about his mother not paying her tab. Nyree's face twisted up at the remark. Ivan wondered what Nyree was thinking. He couldn't make sense of the look. Did the look suggest Ms. Allen was being petty for mentioning the outstanding balance? Or did the look mean that she thought Charity lacked class for not paying her tab?

"How much will this be, Ms. Allen?"

"It's going to be twelve hundred dollars. Yes, these arrangements you selected are not cheap," Ms. Allen smiled and continued, "some of those flowers you chose I am going to have to have them flown in and pay a pretty penny for shipping to ensure that they're here on Wednesday. We have to begin the arrangement process and want everything to be above and beyond what you asked."

Tapping on the class counter, Ivan lowered his head. He was feeling a bit overwhelmed and tired. There was a bottle of Remy 1738 underneath the driver's seat of his Camaro. Vision's of him turning it up to his mouth were filling his head. "Okay, and I'm going to pay my mother's tab too. That Charity was always so forgetful. So fifteen hundred will square everything away," he said.

In a few weeks, money won't be an object. Ivan had reached Shauna Buchanan earlier by phone, and she suggested waiting until the death certificate was received before going through the will. There was nothing she could tell him today as she was on vacation, but would be back in the office Wednesday. He agreed but was going to stop by her office Wednesday. Ivan was consumed with the will and getting the money. It was going to be his anyway, so he wanted to expedite the matter.

"Okay, Little Ivan. You know that's what we used to call you back in the day. My goodness, I haven't seen you in forever. I'm surprised you remembered me. Oh, how is your daddy?" The question had taken him aback. He felt uneasy talking about his father. Everybody in the City of Gary knew Ivan III was a dope addict. Why was she asking? Was she trying to humiliate him? Nyree sensing that Ivan was uneasy spoke up, "He's well. Thanks for asking. Okay, we have the receipt and look forward to seeing a beautiful display on Saturday. Come on Hon, we've got some other matters to handle," Nyree told Ivan as she rushed him out of the store.

"You know what else I got to do?"

"No, what else must you do today?" Nyree asked as her hair blew all over her head due to a gust of wind. They walked down the sidewalk fast to get back to the funeral home parking lot. She looked around the lot and didn't see Ivan's car, but when he stopped at the Camaro parked a few cars down from her Range Rover, Nyree stopped there. "Is this your car?" Nyree asked.

"Yeah, I told you I was letting my boy hold the Mercedes."

"That's crazy. I would've let him hold this and keep rolling the Mercedes. You're a better friend than I am," Nyree rolled her eyes and shook her head in disbelief.

"It's all good. I'm not materialistic and don't get all hung up on money and stuff. It's just money and stuff you can always get that," he told her.

"I guess," she told him not fully believing what she was hearing. The shrug she gave him indicated that if he was okay with it then who was she to find issue with it?

"I have to go to the cemetery. You wanna go?" Ivan asked

"Yikes, not really, but I will for you." she winked at him.

"Okay cool. You would have pissed me off if you would have said, "No." She pissed me off in there asking about my daddy."

"I know. I could tell you weren't feeling that."

"You know me so well," he teased.

"Hm. Do I? What's going on at the cemetery?"

"I already paid for the headstone, but just need to see if I can get mom buried by Gigi. I have to let Tamela know that too."

After leaving the cemetery, Ivan went home and crashed on his sofa. His shoulders were tense. As he propped his hands behind his head, he took a few deep breaths and closed his eyes. Five minutes hadn't passed when repeated knocks at the door caused him to get out of his comfort zone. Peeping through the peephole, he noticed a delivery guy with a bouquet of flowers.

Ivan opened the door. "I'm sure you have the wrong apartment."

"Ivan Marrick IV?" The driver questioned.

"Yeah," Ivan said as he adjusted his black polo.

"Sign for this," the delivery guy said as he handed the Ipad with the signature screen displayed on it.

Ivan snatched the dozen black roses from the man and shut the door. *Somebody is fucking with me, but who and why?*

MALACHI CHANDLER

It was two o'clock in the afternoon and Malachi was sitting in the game room, playing the game system while eating a sandwich. He took a break and picked up his phone to see if he had any notifications, even though it hadn't buzzed to inform him. *Why hadn't Nyree called him back? She said she was just going to the funeral home. It doesn't take this long to make funeral preparations. What if she and that bastard are together, together? Nah, right?*

Malachi was driving himself crazy thinking about what could be keeping Nyree. No messages. No missed calls. Malachi got up to go to the kitchen. He needed something to drink. Cherry Kool-Aid was calling his name in a seductive way. The doctor was on his case about eating properly, drinking more water and all he wanted was Kool-Aid. He laughed at himself. Just as he entered the kitchen, he heard the door chime go off.

"Nyree! Nyree!" He yelled. It was her pet peeve for someone to be yelling in the house, but he did it anyways.

Nyree didn't answer. "Nyree! Ny-ree!" Malachi yelled again as he stirred the Kool-Aid making contents in the pitcher.

"Malachi! Malach!" Nyree yelled as she stood in the kitchen. Her yelling unnerved him as he lost his grip on the pitcher's handle and knocked the pitcher to the floor.

"Damn, see what you made me do?" He looked at her in disbelief.

"I told you about all that hollering in the house. Now, when somebody does it to you, it makes you nervous. I know you better get that mess off my porcelain floor. Put that paper towel down and go get the mop. Aren't you supposed to be drinking more water? Kool-Aid does not meet the water requirement because it's made with water."

Malachi mopped up the mess and shook his head at Nyree. She was really grinding his gears right now.

"You can't call nobody?" Malachi demanded.

"No, I was with him handling business. You said act normal. Plus, you don't know how to talk soft, so he would have heard your voice and then you want details, and I just couldn't talk."

"True, but you could've called me on the way home."

"I could have, but I didn't want to talk on the way home. I just wanted to think. I've been thinking how messed up things are, and I'm usually a good judge of character. I stopped talking to Ivan awhile ago, I should have never… forget it."

"Yeah forget all that going back down memory lane. So what happened?" Malachi was anxiously awaiting details.

Nyree was becoming agitated. It was all in her stance and demeanor. Huffing she said, "Nothing. He paid for his mother's funeral. He's not going to tell his dad that his momma died. He bought some flowers and paid his mother's outstanding balance and we went to the cemetery to figure out where she would be laid to rest. She's going to be placed at her mother's foot."

"Huh?"

"You would have had to have been there to understand it, but I guess where her mother's foot would be in that casket is where the headstone will be placed for Ivan's mother. He's driving a car I've never seen before. It's a Camaro."

"I wonder if his mother had a life insurance policy on him too because I'm going to kill that bastard if he took my money and bought a Camaro," Malachi asked as he began making another pitcher of Kool-Aid. *I hope I get to enjoy this pitcher.*

"I don't think his mother had life insurance."

"Why you say that?" Malachi asked as he poured himself a cup of Kool-Aid.

"Pour me some of that Kool-Aid," Nyree said as she sat at the breakfast bar. "Because he paid for it in cash."

"In cash?" Malachi repeated.

"Yeah, I know I watched them count it out."

"You've got to be kidding me. How much was it?"

"Only the best for mom," Nyree imitated Ivan's voice. Then she continued, "After all was said and done it was about eight thousand."

"So, you mean to tell me he's out here buying cars and burying his mammy with our money. I really can't hear any more," Malachi stormed out of the kitchen and went into the living room. *Let's see what's on television.* There was not much of anything on television of interest so he left the television on a local channel. Malachi picked up People's Magazine and flipped through the pages absently until he got to the article on Prince. He still was having a hard time believing that Prince passed away. Malachi began to reflect on the people who had passed this year and was just thankful he was still in the land of the living.

Nyree came and joined him on the couch with two bowls of ice cream. She smiled at him, "We never got a chance to do this last night," she scooped ice cream onto the tablespoon and put it in his mouth. He returned the favor and fed her ice cream. "I'm so tired I don't know what to do. I've got to start making the last preparations for the kid's Open House."

"When is that going to be again?" Malachi was getting better with remembering things, but he still had moments when it just seemed like he couldn't retain information. Now Ivan Marrick there was nothing he could forget about him. Perhaps because he was obsessed with the man.

"Saturday, June twenty-fifth."

"Okay, and while you planning for the kids don't forget to plan for my birthday."

"Hm," pretending to be confused she said, "when is it again?"

Smacking her knee playfully, his response was, "May twenty-ninth. I swear you play too much."

They were watching "Inside Edition" when a news reporter interrupted, "Live from Gary, Indiana. This is Rob Garnett. Gary, Indiana's talk show host and television station owner, Rayna Summers has been missing for eight weeks. Over the weekend as workers were working along Cline Avenue her remains were found. Dental records confirm that the remains were those of Ms. Summers. She stayed in the spotlight, asked bold questions and had a brief relationship with rapper and best-selling author, Malachi Chandler. Malachi Chandler was the victim of criminal confinement and brutally beaten during that same time frame. Police say that they currently have no people of interest in the case."

"Whoa," Nyree gasped, "are you okay?"

"Yeah, I'm good. That's messed up. I think I'm going to go lie down," Malachi said sullenly.

"Can I get you something?"

"No, I'm good," he told her. *I didn't want to be with her anymore, but I didn't want her dead. This is crazy.* His mind replayed some of his favorite memories with Rayna. He began to wish that he hadn't spoken so harshly to her the last time he saw her. "All I ever wanted was to feel appreciated," she once told him, and now he could hear her voice in his head saying it over and over again. He looked over at Nyree, and she seemed to be in another world. Malachi couldn't help but wonder if she felt guilty about the way she interacted with Rayna the last time she saw her.

"Are you wishing that you hadn't pulled that gun on Rayna? I've been meaning to ask you what got into you on that day."

Nonchalantly, Nyree answered, "Actually, no I do not have any regrets. I hate that she's dead, but that's not my fault. She forced her way in here having a meltdown and I did what I had to do to keep myself and home safe. It's my right to protect my person and property. She came in here unwelcomed and so I wanted her to feel unwelcomed."

"That's really cold, Nyree."

"You asked me, and I told you. Why should I sugar coat it? When I spoke to the police, I didn't sugar coat the situation either. Maybe you should wonder if you weren't always playing the fence between me and her, she would not have come over here acting a fool and put in her place. Now maybe you want to sit around and grieve her loss, but I cannot and will not do it. You can go in that room and shut the door. I'm not going to be made to feel like this is my problem or my fault. I got real problems to address, and your ex is not one."

"You're one to talk about judgments. Look at this fine mess we find ourselves in because of whom you chose to get involved with."

"Seriously, I think we are in this mess because it's a personal thing he has against you. He's always asking about you, how does he measure up to you. It's really kind of eerie when I think about it. Then you act like you don't know him, but he's VIP at Chaotic Bliss. It's your tradition that you meet with each VIP person on the list and take them out to lunch, so how did he get past you? Yeah, that's what I thought. I can hear a spider sneezing."

"Dude is a liar. I don't know him and I don't know how he got on VIP. Nobody at Chaotic Bliss can seem to explain it."

"So, he just pops up out of nowhere and infiltrates himself into our lives. Coincidence. Bull. This was well-crafted and calculated," Nyree tells Malachi as she notices he is not paying attention to her, but the messages coming through on his phone.

"Not today, Nyree, not today. I don't want to do this with you."

" Oh so it's cool for you to talk cash money trash to me all day, but when I call you out on your mess, you don't want to do this with me. This is exactly what I'm talking about. This is the same dance we've been doing for twenty years, and it's gotten old."

"You're right. Your problem is you don't know how to appreciate anyone. If it's not your way you won't acknowledge it. You've got fucked up ways, but you're so narcissistic you can't see it. I love you even though you're flawed. I'm flawed too. I'm not afraid to admit that I'm not perfect but you---you will never fix your mouth to say sorry, I messed up, I made a mistake. You're tired. Me, too. I'm going to get my stuff and go home to my place. It's time."

"Any time you're ready to go you're more than welcome to go. Looks like you can handle yourself, so maybe you should go home. Just hope them fools ain't out there lurking. They never caught anyone if was anyone to catch."

"What? What are you saying?"

"Some of your injuries appeared to be self-inflicted. No one in your neighborhood noticed anything strange or any men, but they did notice Rayna there quite a bit on the day she went missing, and you ended up in your dilemma. Maybe you all fought before she went missing and you couldn't handle what you did…" Nyree was heated.

"It's funny I've been knowing you half my life and to hear you say this stuff is surreal. I would have never imagined you would say nothing like this to me. This is how you really feel. Oh, no words. I can hear a church mouse sneezing. No worries. I'm out of here," Malachi said, disappointed. He didn't want to leave, but Nyree had just insinuated he was capable of murder and would go to lengths to cover it up. He went to his room and began shoving clothes, personal items into suitcases. This whole day had gone awry.

"Daddy where you going with that bag?" India asked as she came through the front door.

"I'm going home."

"Why?" India wanted to know.

"Well, your mother and I just can't seem to coexist under the same roof," he told his daughter.

"That's weird because this weekend you all were all coo-coo for each other and now you all can't coexist? What's really going on? Is it true that Rayna is dead?"

"Your mother knows how to cut people deeply with that mouth of hers and I'm just not going to take it lying down. I had some real goons try to take me out the game. I survived that, but I'm not going to let your mother or anyone tear me down. All my life I've had to prove myself to people. I never had that problem with Nyree, but now, it's like she's different. She's become like the rest of America, and I just can't accept it. Rayna, yeah, she's dead.

I've got people sending me pictures of her remains, and it's really sick and your mother's mouth along with all of this. I can't."

"You know, Daddy, it's not easy for anyone. She was there for you when you were sick. She stayed up nights watching you sleep. I know because I would see her. She camped out for weeks in that chair in your room so that if you coughed in your sleep or missed a breath in your sleep she'd be right there. Never complained about it. I would hear her praying fervently for you. Sometimes we'd walk past the room, and she'd be at the foot on her knees, head bowed praying. Lips be moving, but no words coming out. That's that "get down prayer" Grandma Lula be talking about. So, I'm saying you know how she is, but that don't mean she doesn't love you. And speaking of a slick mouth, you're not half-stepping," India told her dad.

"You done?"

"Yeah, I'm done. See what I mean? That sarcasm, you both do it all the time," India spoke freely.

"I hear you," he told his daughter as he wheeled the suitcase back to his room.

With India on his heels, she continued speaking, "Yeah you hear me, but are you listening? Take it in and let it marinate like seasoning."

"A'ight Nikki Minaj. I heard you. I heard you."

"I've got the craziest parents in America. Ya'll love each other, but then every time life is about to be all good for y'all, one of you go and do something to sabotage it. But no, not this time. Me and Christian have sat back and watched this repeated pattern of behavior, and this can't be healthy to you all, but it's not healthy for us. See, I personally don't want to end up getting in jacked up relationships because of my parents' behavior. So, you all get off that roller coaster today. It's really okay to be happy. It's okay to be drama free. Real talk you all are too old to be carrying on like this. I got to go do my homework and then I'm hanging out tonight. Ya'll make somebody wanna go smoke something," India told her father as she adjusted her ponytail.

"What you mean smoke something? Let me find out you been smoking."

"Really, Daddy, I don't smoke, but come on think about all the dysfunction me and Christian have been subjected to, could you blame us. I mean you guys have not really been around for us emotionally this year. Now, we're old enough to know right from wrong, but if we had gotten off into some boo-type stuff, you guys would not know."

Malachi was in the process of getting ready to respond but noticed that India was reading a text, and it had her eyes swelling with tears. "What's wrong with you?"

"Ivan just sent me a text saying that his mother lost her battle to cancer and could me and Christian keep him in our prayers. We got so much to be thankful for, wow, I can't even imagine. When you were in the hospital, that was scary. Christian and I weren't sure if you were going to make it at first. I'm just thankful," she hugged her dad.

"I love you, Baby."

"I love you too, Daddy. If you love someone you should tell them and do what it takes to keep them in your life, you know?"

"When did you get to be so wise?"

"I've always been like this. I just never really expressed myself."

"Go handle your business. I will see you later," Malachi said as he walked out of the room and toward the front door, "I got some business to handle. I said I will see you later. Don't look like that, I will be back."

"Bye Malachi," he heard Nyree call from a distance.

"It's not bye, I will see you later, and you better be ready," he yelled.

"Stop hollering in the house, you know..." Nyree yelled, and Malachi shut the door on it.

It would be easy to walk away from Nyree and the children and go back home. He could blame life and circumstances for his situation. The ordeal he had endured could be a crutch to excuse his behavior. India was right, he and Nyree needed to get their acts together. Malachi sprinted up the stairs and knocked on Nyree's closed bedroom door.

"Yes," she answered through the door.

He knocked again. Her response was the same. He knocked again. She swung the door open with an attitude and asked, "What?"

"You need to quit being so mean. I got to go handle some business, and when I come back, we need to talk."

"Say what you going to say now," she exhaled.

"All I'm going to say now is I love you. I got to go handle this business, and I will be back. You be ready to listen," he told her and ran down the hallway and then down the stairs.

Officer Morrison had sent him a text telling him that he had heard that Malachi was going to be brought in for questioning in the murder of Rayna Summers. Before he would let officers and media come to the house, he decided to go down to the station and talk to the officers. There was nothing to hide. He was as much a victim as Rayna was a victim.

After two and a half grueling hours, Malachi was finally dismissed from the police station. On his way past the front desk, he noticed Ivan Marrick IV was there and telling the officer that he was the victim of a stalking. Malachi mumbled loud enough for Ivan and the officer to hear him say, "God don't like ugly."

"What's that the officer asked?"

"Nothing. I was really talking to myself," Malachi shrugged, made eye contact and winked at Ivan.

IVAN MARRICK

It had been the most chaotic and draining week of Ivan's life. Walking to his car in the parking lot of Guy & Allen he sighed. The wake had been too much to endure. He wondered where he would pull the strength from to handle tomorrow. Nyree had shown up and stayed for a while. Ivan didn't think there was a person in Gary, Indiana that she didn't know. Having her there had really taken some stress off of him. Ivan kept fantasizing about what it would be like to be married to her. Malachi had his chance, and he blew it. He didn't deserve happiness. Everything he loves should be taken from him just as it had been taken from Ivan. Ivan still blamed his father's drug addiction on Malachi and as a result of his father's drug addiction, Ivan lost everything.

As Ivan positioned himself in the front seat, he reached under the driver's seat and retrieved the brown paper bag that he had stashed there earlier. Disappointment loomed over him as he thought about the bottle Tamela had confiscated from him when he walked into the funeral home. He was glad that he had this backup bottle. Hurriedly, he unfastened the cap and took a few quick swigs from the bottle. "AHHH!" That burn going down was vicious. Taking another swig from the bottle, he shook his head in disbelief as he thought about yesterday.

Ivan had seen Attorney Shauna Buchanan yesterday, and they went through the will. Ivan snickered at the thought. There was nothing in the will of significance. His mother had left everything to his father, and his father was the only beneficiary on the insurance policy that he was not aware that she had. There was a letter she left, and it said she had given him everything in life. She had signed over her shares of the construction company to him and hoped he had been prosperous. Ivan laughed at the thought. He had sold his shares of the company to get quick money. Where had the money gone? He wished he had an idea, but he didn't. Nothing to show for it. Sitting in the car, he felt sick. Onyx had been texting him about paying up. You can't pay what you don't have. Ivan began driving but was not focused on the road or the vehicles on the road.

Fresh out of Xanax, he was not sure how he would cope. It would be nice if he would go to sleep and not wake up. Suicide, he thought about it, but he was too scary to attempt it. Ivan sped home in his sport's car. Not sure what he was in a rush for because when he got to the door of his apartment, his stalker's calling card was there. A dozen black roses. There were three dozen black roses in a bouquet at the funeral home. The ribbon indicated that they were from a "Close Friend."

They had mom looking good. She looked peaceful. Her hair looked good too. Her money green dress look good in the coffin. I can't believe she left me nothing. She left everything to a man who never put her first. I put my life on hold for her and got nothing. Wow! Ivan found himself thinking as he lay in bed and finally sleep fell upon him.

The next morning, Ivan awoke, and his heart pumped harder than he ever remembered. Ivan felt the worst type of pain rivet through his body. When people describe losing people close to them and how it felt like a piece of themselves had been ripped out of their body, he now literally knew what they were talking about. Ivan poured himself some R&R, Remy Martin, and Red Bull. There were certain occasions that demanded R&R and today was such an occasion. The funeral car arrived as scheduled at Ivan's apartment. He had no idea how he would get home. Perhaps Nyree would bring him home after the repast. He hoped she would not frown about the fact that it was being held at a local nightclub. *Hell, this was how he wanted to remember his mother's life in the form of a party, so forget what she and any of the critics had to say. I sure hope my daddy doesn't show up here today.*

All eyes were on Ivan, as he stepped out of the limousine. Ivan paused and watched the onlookers through his Tom Ford shades. He stood on the sidewalk and just let the onlookers view him. Ivan knew he was looking good. *I'm Hollywood status everywhere I go. They can't help but want to see me.* He was wearing a money green button down Ralph Lauren polo shirt, khaki pants, and money green Ralph Lauren shoes. The seats were filled in the sanctuary as he walked down the aisle to view his mother's body on last time. As he was walking up the aisle, Nyree was walking down the aisle toward him. He smiled as they walked toward each other. *She is wearing that money green dress. Wonder why her arms are behind her back.*

"Hey Sweetie," he whispered as he hugged her.

Nyree stood there with a smirk on her face. She didn't say anything. Then as if she suddenly remembered something she said, "Oh, I have something for you," pulling her hands to her sides. Her right hand contained two black roses. She handed one to Ivan and kept walking down the aisle. Then she walked to the casket and put the other black rose on Charity's chest. Ivan stood in shock as he watched Nyree walked on the outer aisle and take a seat in the rear. The funeral director approached Ivan and led him into the hallway so that the funeral could begin. As if it were not enough to be presented with the rose from Nyree, Malachi suddenly appears out of nowhere.

Too close for Ivan's comfort, Malachi had invaded his personal space. "What up man?" Not waiting for a response, Malachi gives Ivan a side hug and whispers in his ear, "You messed with the wrong man and his wife."

"Your ex, you mean," Ivan said.

"Mr. Marrick, we need to get started," the funeral director told him.

"In a minute," Ivan told the older distinguished gentleman. Turning his attention back to Malachi he saw the smile on his face that had him uneasy.

"You didn't notice that engagement ring on her finger. Ex only refers to you. I'm here present and future, but don't let me hold you up. You've got to get this show on the road."

Ivan gestured as if he wanted to throw a punch at Malachi. Malachi laughed, "This ain't what you want. You thought it was, but you made a bad decision. Let me go find Nyree. I wouldn't miss this for the world. Oh and I'm sorry for your losses."

"Mr. Marrick…"

"Yeah, I'm ready. Let's do this." *This is what we on now. Malachi Chandler and Nyree really came here and did this.*

Ivan walked down the aisle with very few members of his family following behind him. He was happy to finally be able to take his seat. If his nosy auntie asked him one more time what that scene was about with Malachi, he would die. Finally, he had to turn and say, "Sh… I will tell you after the service." His cousin whom he hadn't seen in over fifteen years kept whispering, "You okay?" *Nah, I'm not okay. How did people think he would be with the passing of his mother and all the other matters facing him?*

After the service was over, Ivan noticed Malachi and Nyree being very cozy. Ivan decided to walk over to them. In mid-step, he felt a huge presence come over him. He couldn't describe it. Then he heard a male voice ask as he was being tapped on his shoulder, "Ivan Marrick IV?"

Not turning to look, with his arrogance he assumed it was someone who wanted to console him or interview him for a news story, he said, "Yeah, but not right now."

Then he felt his arms being pulled behind his back and then he saw officers in front of him. The crowd had gotten larger. "Ivan

Marrick IV, you're being arrested for check fraud, forgery, grand theft auto, burglary, and a suspect in the murder and disappearance of Rayna Summers. You have the right to remain silent..."

What the hell? This is not happening. This is not happening at my mother's funeral. I know Nyree is not over there smiling. I can't tell if she's smiling with these shades on. I think she's laughing at me. Who is she? This is not the woman I fell for. No, that's not my Nyree. All these charges I'm facing. What am I going to do? I'm not cut out for jail.

"Ya'll ain't got to do all this," Ivan complained as he was pushed into the back of a squad car. *Damn, I wanted to send mom off and have a memorable service, but not like this.*

CHAOS - Nyree Chandler

This one individual
Is something like a smooth criminal.
He stole my heart,
From the very start.

I gave him my all and all,
He got me checking my caller id a million times
Just to see if he called.
He pretended to be tough
Gave him my all
But it was never enough…

Loved him more than life
Loved to hear him call me "wife."
Never wanted the drama,
Didn't sign up to have to constantly address a baby momma.

We're like fire and ice,
He makes me mad and it's nothing nice.
Wish there were a drug
To flush him out of my system.
It doesn't exist.
I guess chaos is bliss.

About the Author

Jahzara is a Gary, Indiana native. Her writing journey began when she was in the third grade. She recalls that it started when she was placed in the "Wee-One's" corner after having one too many confrontations with the boys in the classroom. Her third grade teacher really thought that she was punishing Jahzara by putting her in the "Wee-One's" corner and separating her from the rest of the class. Jahzara wishes to thank Mrs. Smith for providing her with the composition books and her own space in the classroom to be creative.

Jahzara is the author of *The Love She Longed For* series, *Contradictions, Never Would Have Made It: A Testimony of What God Has Done In My Life, The Diva's Dating Assessment Tool: Girl, PLEASE!* She was one of the contributing authors in best-selling author, Shannon Holmes' anthology: *Hood2Hood.* Jahzara has written for Soulful Nights Blog. Additionally, she has hosted two radio shows, "Monday Madness" and "It's Complicated."

Jahzara is an educator, writer for hire, and Clinical Massage Therapist.

Jahzara is a creative being. Not only does she express herself in written form she does it through her t-shirt line as well, which coincides with her philosophy, "When I couldn't find the experience I was looking for in life, I created it." Additionally, she has created her own fragrance line, Tranquil Bliss and custom creates fragrances for others. Stay in contact with her @jahzarabradley on Instagram as well as:

chaoticblissfragrance.blogspot.com

www.facebook.com/jahzarab

twitter.com/mzjahzara

Heat Meter

• Heat Meter- stories that I write in response to a writing prompt to see if I still can bring that heat in my writing.

Writing Prompt: Write about a rich, attractive woman.

Rich Attractive Woman

   Gia clutched the steering wheel of her BMW for dear life as she set in the parking lot of Starbucks. She was shaking uncontrollably as her mind replayed what happened a block ago. "You stupid imbecile," she remembered yelling at the snow plow driver who had swerved into her lane from the opposite side of the road and then back into its lane. Her life flashed before and in that moment she realized she was not ready to die. Gia had to compose herself in the parking lot. After the warmth of the heated seat began to fade away, she decided to open the car door. Two inches of snow on ground was not a lot of snow, but add in the wind chill of three below zero Gia found it hard to walk. It was good thing she worked out three to four times a week. She was drawing on all the strength in her thighs to walk in the four inch heels. Her ears were freezing as she trekked to the door. Gia could not risk messing up her freshly done curly locks. Besides she was meeting with important clients this morning and messy hair and below zero temperatures were no reason for not to be on top of her game. Pulling on the door, she nearly lost her balance. Soon as she stepped in the threshold, she became aware of her surroundings. There were people occupying every table, sofa, love seat and the line was just about ending where she stood. Gia contemplating leaving. *I came this far, I'm not turning around. I'm not a quitter. However, I don't have time for this,* she found herself thinking. Looking at her Tag Heuer timepiece, she literally did not have time for this. In less than an hour, she had to make a presentation to the General Manager of Hilton Hotels. This was a deal that was going to have her sitting pretty financially. Gia, brushed past the people in line and walked up to a Caucasian man, six foot three wearing a cashmere coat. As he placed his order, she interlocked arms with him and before he could protest, she leaned into him and whispered in his ear, "Just do as I say and it will be okay."

Gia felt him tense up. "I will make it worth your while," she winked at him and then turned to the cashier, "yes, and I'm going to have a mocha caramel latte and a bagel. Just charge it to the Tranquil Moments business account."

The man stood in awe. "What's your name, Sweetie?" Gia asked.

"Br...Brian," he said.

"Brian, what's wrong? You looked surprised that a beautiful black woman would buy you coffee."

"No, um yes, I...I'm not sure what's happening here." Gia smiled as she broke the arm lock and moved closer to the counter.

"Carlos, it's been one hell of a morning and it's not even nine o'clock yet. I want to buy everyone's coffee this morning that is in line from here to the man back there with the black Colombia coat. Cap me off at three hundred dollars though," she told the cashier.

"Of course, Ms. Black, he responded."

"And give yourself a forty dollar tip but I need that mocha caramel latte like yesterday."

Gia reached into her coat pocket and handed Brian her business card. She turned to him and said, "If you want to have more fun call me. "

"Ms. Black your order is ready."

Gia grabbed her order and strolled out of Starbucks without looking back.

Creating a Scene:

Rayna rolled her eyes at Ivan when she finally saw his face. It had taken him forever and a day to open the door to his 3,000 square foot home on Lake Michigan. He couldn't move fast enough to allow her to enter the door. Trembling as she took off her boots at the front door, she wondered where she would place them. The mat that held boots and shoes was completely full, in fact over flowing. As she stood up and removed her gloves, her fingers seemed to be numb. She brought her hands up to her mouth and allowed her warm breath to bring life back to her fingers. *I hope I don't have frost bite,* she found herself thinking. Her heart was beating fast. It was too bad she could not attribute the anxiety to frigid, below zero February temperatures. *What in the hell is going on here? I can't even find a hook to hang my coat. Forget it, I will just hang my coat in the closet.* Rayna could not believe all the paper and items stuffed into the coat closet. A book fell off the shelf and missed her head by inches. *Damn, Ivan, what is really going on? For him to be OCD, this is ridiculous.*

Rayna finally made her way to the living room after circling around, bags in the floor. Ivan was sprawled out on the red leather sectional sofa she had picked out a few years ago. "Move over and let me sit down," she told him. Looking up at her, he shook his head to indicate that was not going to happen. Sighing, she lifted his legs, sat down and allowed his legs to rest on her thighs. He slid up and down on the sofa to get comfortable and wiggled his toes.

"You feisty tonight. What's up with you, Sweetness?"

Defensively she answered, "What you mean what's up with me? Who said something was up with me?" Rayna was nervous and she knew that word traveled fast in Gary, Indiana. Everybody knew everybody pretty much or if not that somebody who knew somebody who knew somebody. As she tried to avoid his question she noticed several empty beer cans and red Styrofoam cups on the coffee table. On the entertainment center was a lonely bottle of Hennessy black with what appeared to be half a swallow remaining in it. There were empty to-go-containers from Gowdy's Fishery on the bar. There was marijuana residue on the coffee table which would explain the stench of marijuana in the air.

"Sweetie, you got a problem. You never show up without calling first unless there's a problem. Did you lose your house keys again? You know where your spare keys are. You can go get them or spend the night and we could…"

"Ivan, is that all you think about? Looks like you've done enough of that tonight."

"We got a don't ask don't tell policy but if you must know, I got it in with two twin sisters last night and when I tell you…"

"Too much info," she told him as she rushed down the hallway to the bathroom. "I got to pee," she yelled to him as she slammed the door. She nearly tripped over his shoes as she walked to the toilet. The roll of toilet paper was barely existent and was that a used condom floating in the toilet. Rayna was beyond disgusted.

When she returned to the living room, she told Ivan, "Your home is a wreck…you could've at least cleaned the bathroom."

Annoyed by her statement, he replied, "Had I known I was going to have guests at three in the morning I'm sure I would've tidied up a bit."

Rayna shrugged her shoulders. "So, I came by to let you know that it is over with me and Malachi. He decided that he wants to go back and make things work with his ex wife."

Ivan bolted up as if lightning had struck him. "Nah, nah, that can't be. You got to salvage this relationship. If you all break up that will ruin everything we've worked so hard for."

Rayna smirked. "We. Dammit, I'm the only one who's been working, you have just been reaping the benefits."

Writing Prompt: Include in your story the following line: By noon her coffee was untouched and cold and when 5:00 came she was tired with red puffy eyes.

As Gia unlocked the door, she found herself thinking that she had never been so happy to be home. This had been the craziest day ever. She went from waking up at her usual time for work to running late for the bus. By noon her coffee was untouched and cold and when 5:00 came she was tired with red puffy eyes. Shutting and locking the door, she sauntered into living room and stared at the clock. It was five o'clock and she felt dead dog tired. She could not wait for Taboo to call her. She was going to read him the riot act. Why in the hell did she have to catch the bus and she had a car? He was the cause of her car getting impounded. Oh, yes he had a lot of explaining to do. Did she really want to hear what he had to say? Gia found herself looking in the mirror to see if she looked as bad as she felt. She frowned at her reflection. Horrible was about the nicest word she could use to describe what she saw. Make-up was pretty much nonexistent and the Visine eyedrops had done nothing to conceal the fact she cried herself to sleep on and off all night. She heard the words of her late mother play out in her head, "If a person lived to be one hundred years old and you spent every waking moment with him/her you will never know that person." As a kid she just thought her mother was real old school and did not know what she was talking about. The words of the wise woman seemed to ring true.

Gia nestled herself onto the leather sofa in the living room and laughed nervously. It was a coping mechanism because nothing was funny. Her stomach growled. She had not eaten since this time yesterday. Generally, she did not eat breakfast. Her daily coffee usually tided her over until lunch at noon. Her stomach had been in knots all day and she had no desire to eat or drink anything. Last night around ten o'clock the police had come to her house with a search warrant to search the house. Taboo had left out around seven-thirty saying that he had to go check on his night club that he owned. There was a situation, she heard him discussing in a low tone on his cell phone. Gia thought he would have been back by ten so when she heard pounding on the door, she assumed he had left his keys at home as usual. To her surprise it was members of the Gary Response Investigative Team with a search warrant. Apparently this FBI led team had been watching Taboo and he was one of the most wanted drug dealers in Lake County Indiana. They sounded like drones when they spoke and rummaged through her belongings. Nothing turned up. Taboo had been shot in a drug deal gone wrong in an upscale subdivision. After they left her home, she rushed to the Methodist Hospitals Northlake campus to see Taboo. He was under heavy guard and very sedated. Gia was certain that he knew she was there. He looked at her with a piercing stare. "Taboo, what the hell is going on?"

"The hills have eyes. We shall eat bread soon," he told her. This was code language for their people listening but we will talk soon.

Gia found herself on the sofa crying. Taboo had been removed from intensive care and transported to Lake County Jail earlier today. Last week his car had been totaled and he had driven her car to the mysterious errand last night and it was in police custody. Never in a million years could she have dreamed that the man she loved, shared her bed with for the past two years was a drug lord. They lived well but not flashy. Things were starting to make sense now. He had set up several accounts in her son's name. The flip cell phone. Gia shook her head as she pulled a blanket over her and reclined on the couch. Her head was throbbing again.

Writing Prompt: Incorporate the following line in your writing: It's not that simple. You think I'm going to just let you walk out my life again.

Back From the Dead

"Hi, welcome to Starbuck. What can I get you?" The cheery blonde haired teenage girl asked.

Gia rolled her eyes. It was just a little past eight and Gia had not fully awakened but this little teeny bopper's energy was fueling Gia. She beamed at the girl and said, "Good morning, I am going to have a Caramel Macchiato Venti with an…"

"With an iced lemon pound cake, it's not good for me but…" Taboo Washington stood behind Gia saying.

Gia froze and did not move. Nobody in the world could finish that statement but the love of her life, Taboo. That voice belonged to Taboo. Gia could not move. It had been over a year since she had seen him alive. He had escaped from Lake County Jail, while being handcuffed to a bed in the infirmary section of the jail. Taboo had been on the run for weeks. The media had a field day with the story and dubbed him "The Black Houdini. When police finally captured him he allegedly had an arsenal of weapons and they had no choice but to kill him "I'm going to have a Caramel Macchiato Tall, she is all the sweetness I need in my life," he told the cashier. "You're all the sweetness I need," is a statement that Taboo often told her. The voice sounded like his with a tinge of sadness. Turning around to face the man, she looked and saw a man who favored Taboo but he looked older.

Standing there a whole foot taller than her with his hands in his freshly starched jeans, he whispered, "Hey My Love." Before she could respond he showered her with a sensual hug that allowed him to caress her glutes. Then he kissed her as if this were part of their daily ritual. Gia could have sworn she saw tiny stars after the magical kiss as she inhaled his signature cologne, Dat Dude. It was just like old times. He looked older, more distinguished. There was graying around the temples, his face was slightly worn but not wrinkled. She tried to search his eyes to see if they would tell her a story. He immediately broke the gaze. Gia could tell he was more guarded than he had been in their previous lifetime "I will get our order. Go grab our favorite table," he stated.

As she set at the table in the rear, she watched him. She pinched herself to make sure this was real. After a few moments of standing at the counter he joined her at the table.

"You don't look happy to see me," he joked.

Gia reached across the table and slapped him.

He held his jaw for a moment and she noticed his well-manicured nails. Taboo always kept his nails manicured and clean. "Gia, damn, what was that for?"

"Are you freaking kidding me? You're dead. I buried you. I spent the last of my savings to put you away nicely. I went to your funeral. I've cried for months and mourned your death. I come here every morning just like we used to before I went to the office. And then you show up today like this is what we do! Nah."

"Keep your voice down. The hills still do have eyes. I know your pain. I've watched you for months come in here. I've seen you sit here and have a melt down and then pull yourself together before driving off to work. I had to leave like I did to protect you."

"Protect *me*. Protect me from what? Everything about you was a lie. You never owned that nightclub, you had shares in it but you made it seem like you were sole owner. I lost everything because of you. I had to downgrade to a smaller home, the car was seized, bank accounts frozen…"

"Look, I still can't get into all of it. The night I left I told you I had a serious situation at the club. You acting like you didn't know what I did. I met you through your brother. Come on now, birds of a feather flock together. That's all I'm going to say. If I didn't vanish, they were going to kill you and Kenny. I didn't want to leave you but I had to. I love you that much. I violated the codes of the street and the feds helped me. They orchestrated everything. They wanted me but who I gave them made me seem like the bottom rung of the food chain."

"The funeral, escape from jail all that was fake too?" Gia cried.

"Sweetheart, I am going to suggest you forget everything about that. You're doing well. Enjoy life. Enjoy that company you're running. Remember this, you have what you have because I allow you to have it. In a minute your life can be turned upside down again. You really should be thanking me instead of playing this 'I'm so much better than you role'. Be good." He kissed on the cheek and got up to leave. Gia grabbed him by the arm and forced his to sit down.

"It's not that simple. You think I'm going to just let you walk out my life again. The last time I saw you, you were in critical condition at Methodist Hospital. Then you went to jail and would not put me on your visiting list. No stay awhile. Let's sip coffee and talk. You came back in my life for a reason and I want to know why."

Heat Meter- Random Writing

Nyree ran through the automatic door of the Lake County Jail dripping wet. The wind had turned her umbrella inside out and that last sprint caused her to twist her right ankle. It was throbbing. This was her bad ankle, the one she fractured years ago. *Please, oh, please do not be injured. I don't need anymore chaos in my life. Damn these dollar sale flip flops. I should have known better.* The flip flops from Old Navy had no support but they were cute and she prided herself on being well put together. *This probably was not the day to wear those flip flops.* Wiping her face with a crumpled tissue, she retrieved from her purse she sighed. Her visit was set to start in seven minutes. This was not her first time visiting an inmate but it was her first time using the computer to schedule it. *It's not too late to leave. Yep, I could tell him it was a tornado warning I decided not to come. It is a tornado set to come this way. Forget it, I'm here. Traveled through hell to get here so I will do my thirty minute visit and if it does not go well I never have to come back.*

Her name was at the top of the digital screen announcing visitors and inmates. *Oh my gosh, I did not know that they put you all out like that when you visit an inmate. I should have registered under an assumed name.* Quickly she remembered that was not possible because you had to provide a copy of your driver's license to set up your Telmate account. *I hope I don't see anyone I know here.* She reached into her purse and searched for one of her prepaid credit cards that did not have her name on it. This was a card she used when she was doing something that she did not want traced back to her. There was no need to have a jail visitation linked to her financial statements. *Malachi would have a fit if he knew I came here. I just need closure with Ivan, that's the only reason I'm here.*

"Hi," she smiled at the male correctional officer who was looking at her through the glass at the counter. Nyree found herself wondering how thick the glass was as he pressed a button to greet her. *He's looking rather fine and he works out. He could handcuff me anytime.*

"Can I help you?" He asked politely.

"Uh huh," Nyree said staring at him. Nothing came out of her mouth.

Waving his hand as if to say, "Out with it." He smiled at her.

"Yes, this is my first time doing the Telmate visit and I needed to pay for the visit but I don't know how. I was wondering if you could tell me how to go about doing it."

"Who are you visiting today?"

She drew closer to the glass and whispered, "Ivan Marrick."

The officer turned a few pages and looked up at her.

"Don't say he can't have visits today after all I've been through to get here," she demanded as she adjusted her wet hair to allow it to drape behind her shoulders. Her close were soaking wet and sticking to her. She looked around the lobby and observed that most of the people there were soaking wet.

"No, it's not that. He has not had any visitors this week. His first visit of the week is free so no worries. You've been assigned booth 3. It looks like you're set to start your visit in about one minute. You log into the system the same way you do from home."

"Oh," Nyree said disappointed. She was hoping that she would get to see Ivan in person but it was going to be a real time video visit. Her heart was pounding as she walked to her small cubicle. She felt saddened to see families huddled in cubicles around a screen trying to talk to their loved one as one person passed the phone to another.

Finally, Ivan appeared on the screen wearing black and white prison uniform. His hair was uncut and had grown into a small afro. There was a fresh scar over his eye.

"Hey Baby Girl. I was surprised when you sent me a visit request. What brings you here? Did you come to gloat?"

"No, you know we had some great moments together and I really just wanted to make sure you were okay."

"Yeah, I'm good," he said looking down and avoiding making eye contact with her.

"Hey, I didn't come here to look at your head. Look up and talk to me, we don't have long to talk."

"Nyree, what do you want. You didn't come here to make sure I was okay. You could have sent me a message to find that out. So, let's cut the shit and get to it. You know at anytime I can discontinue this visit," he told her as if he were running thing.

"Ivan, I just have so many questions. Us was there really an "us" or was your motivation for getting close to me more to get at Malachi?"

"Now, that's more like it, Nyree. Getting to the nitty gritty. What we had was real but your ex-husband has been a thorn in my side for a long time and I just went about it the wrong way."

"You think? You had him kidnapped and left for dead while you whisked me off to Florida."

"We had fun in Florida and you know it. Besides I provided you with an alibi. You were the first one they suspected but your alibi was solid."

"You wanted me to be a suspect to save your ass. Why did you have him kidnapped?"

"I don't know what you're talking about. I don't get down like that."

"You just said you did."

"No, I said our trip to Florida provided you with an alibi."

"You admitted you went about it the wrong way."

"I went about trying to gain your affection and take your mind off Malachi the wrong way. Nyree, you've never been a match for me. I've always been able to outthink you. I'm five steps ahead of you. Whoever sent you sent you here on a bullshit mission. You're failing miserably. This is what you can go back and tell them. The State of Indiana has nothing on me. They've wrongfully denied me bail. The charges are bullshit and I'm going to beat this case. I got the best lawyer money can buy. When I go to court Monday, I will be out of here and all of you who crossed me should be very afraid. I was saddened to hear about that fire that started at your grandmother's house. I've been here 21 days, but I still get things done in the streets."

"My mistake for coming here. I thought from the text we've had you were getting your life together. All those scriptures you were quoting and everything had me fooled. You better change your ways before someone else does. It's your choice," she shrugged. "You can continue with your worthless life, or you can become someone who matters."

Writing Prompt: She added a charm to her bracelet for every life that she took

Sweet Treats

Gia Black nearly tripped over the industrial mat in between of the double doors of Jared's Jewelry store. The weight of the door sent her for a jolt. Regaining her composure quickly, she found herself face to face with the store manager, Ian Christenson. This man was the sexiest man of Oriental decent she had seen. His suit hung off his body as if it were tailor made. Gia liked the finer things in life and this man was fine. She smooth her fitted dress over her voluptuous hips and smiled her million dollar smile as she ran her fingers through her short haircut wondering why she had gotten it cut. Smirking at the thought, she remembered it was easier for her to get her job done and not have to worry about the maintenance of it. It was curled now but when she was putting in work she could care less about how her hair looked. In fact, she wore a wig when she was putting in work. No traces of evidence to be left at the scenes of the crimes.

"Gia, you were just in last week. Back so soon?" Ian questioned.

Smiling, she responded, "Ian, I love the way you take care of me. You know I gotta have my sweet treats."

"Can I get you a latte?"

"No, not today. It's hot outside."

It was ninety-eight degrees and if she wanted a latte she would have one despite the temperature but her reference was regarding the police who were looking for a serial killer in Northwest Indiana. Gia covered her tracks well until last month in July she knocked off three people and just here in the month of August and it was just the eighth day she had already killed two people.

"That's never stopped you before, the heat…" Ian said.

"Yes, I know but sometimes you got to change things up. And I'm not feeling it today. But how about you pull up my wish list and tell me what the next charm is on my list and tell me what ice product is next for me to purchase."

"Ice, you know you are my only customer who refers to diamonds as ice," he said while scrolling through her wish list items on his Ipad. "Okay, your next charm is the musical note, oh wait it says combine the musical note with the violin and wow, for ice, you're getting a pair of three carat earrings."

"Indeed," she winked. Ian had her order correct.

"You're into music. I never took you for the music type," Ian said.

"I appreciate music. Into music, I guess you could say that I used to be into it. Well such is life," she sighed.

As Ian wrapped up the items he commented, "It's a shame about what happened to the music professor at the university."

"Hm, what's that?"

"Surprised you haven't seen on the news about the professor who was found strangled with some homemade device containing guitar strings, cable, and some other stuff. Pretty scary, huh."

"Wow, I hadn't heard that. Sounds scary."

"Crime of passion they're calling it. They said he must have known his attacker, no signs of forced entry. Your total $6,890 with tax."

Gia didn't flinch as she paid in cash. A crime of passion, huh, that's what they're calling it. Professor Newton got what he had coming to him. For years he had played me like a violin. Told me he loved me and we were going to be together forever. He failed to mention that he was in love with his gay lover and that he just wanted to experience sex with an unsuspecting, naïve black girl. Well, seeing them entangled in his sheets woke me up and I had to end the nightmare. Every time, I kill I add a new charm to my bracelet. Gia looked at the charm she had just added to her bracelet and nodded in approval.

"Okay, Ian, my love, thanks so much and as always it was good seeing you."

"See you soon," he said as she walked away.

"Definitely. You will definitely be seeing me soon," she said as she walked out of the jewelry store thinking about who the next person would be to receive elimination notice.

Green Chai Tea Latte

Every step was a grueling one as she approached the booth in the rear of The Blueberry Spoon. It was an upscale restaurant in the beach community of Gary, Indiana. When she finally made it to her booth, Nyree Chandler sighed. Although, she was a beautiful and intelligent woman, being in her early fifties was beginning to catch up with her. Six years ago, she could have worn six inch heels all day and not thought about her feet. But today, her feet, toes and hamstrings were screaming, "Bloody murder!" Glad that the waitress had scurried off to get her a caramel latte, she let her feet slip out of her heels. Her black dress was a little snug through her hips. What in the hell was going on with her? She knew damn well what the problem was-- potatoes, chocolate, bread and not spending time in the gym. Tight dress. Tight shoes. And just this morning she swore she had seen five new strands of gray hair around her temple. Her caramel complexion was still smooth as a baby's behind. Not a wrinkle in sight. This could not be happening... getting old. Nyree always had been concerned about her weight and her appearance and now it seemed nature and age were taking over. Nyree was used to being in control of every aspect of her life but the age process she could not control. Two weeks ago, her son announced that he and his fiancé were expecting a child. Somebody was going to be calling her grandma in a few year and that added to her anxiety.

Her phone vibrated and she saw the icon indicating she had a text message. Some good news, she was hoping to read. It was Malachi, her husband. "Hey Babe, just made it to the airport. I can't wait to get home. If you need to beef up security do it. The trip wasn't what I thought it would be. I will tell you about it when I get home."

Shaking her head, she mumbled to no one in particular, "I told you going to Miami to hear that little youngster rap was going to be a waste of time. His flow and bars were not unique." Rolling her eyes she thought about the time and money they had wasted on the juvenile rapper, Donut.

The cheery waitress set a mug on the table and asked if she could take Nyree's order. "Not right now. Give me a moment," Nyree smiled and tried to sound as pleasant as she could. Just yesterday, Ivan Marrick, her former love interest had been released from prison . Ivan had Malachi kidnapped and left for dead. In addition to that he had stolen over fifty thousand dollars from the couple. Her nerves were on edge. She did not want to go home to an empty house. The thought of Ivan being free was unsettling. He couldn't stay in prison forever but why did his release have to get released while Malachi was gone. Malachi would be home soon, she knew it but things could get really ugly in Gary, Indiana in a matter of minutes. Nyree recalled receiving a letter from Ivan in which he wrote "Wait 'til I get free." She took it as a threat. Prison officials laughed it off as a love letter from an ex.

Nyree turned her attention to the mug. She stared at her favorite green tea chai latte that set beside her and frowned. "Hey Anna," she shouted to her waitress, "I didn't order this." Before Anna could respond she heard, "True, but I did," the chilling voice of Ivan reached her ears before he sat down in front of her. "Hello again."

Swallowing hard, her voice cracked, "What are you doing here?"

Ivan's green eyes squinted at her. He cleaned up well for someone who had just spent the last ten years in prison. "Hey My Love, I know you can greet me better than that. Last time I saw you was at my mother's funeral and I was getting carted off to jail. Did you miss me?" he asked as he reached across the table and stroked her face. "Your skin is still soft."

"Don't touch me ."

Ivan laughed. "Used to be a time when you couldn't get enough of this touch."

Nyree threw the tea in his face, slid her feet into her heels and strode out of the restaurant with style and grace.

Order this inspirational title from Tranquil Moments. *Never Would Have Made It: A Testimony of What God Has Done In My Life*. Things are accomplished when people exercise their faith, and tap into their courage to become better, wiser and stronger.

Crazy Faith - Anthology

The difference between your current state and where you want to be is *Crazy Faith*. Crazy Faith is an anthology composed of inspirational and feel good stories by eleven authors that will help you do more than survive but thrive. This is the year that you live your ideal life. Decree and declare what you want manifested in your life, plant your crazy faith seeds and watch the fruit manifest.

www.ingramcontent.com/pod-product-compliance
Lightning Source LLC
Chambersburg PA
CBHW070324260626
47160CB00003B/941